UNDER
– THE –
NEON
LIGHTS

UNDER
- THE -
NEON
LIGHTS

Arriel Vinson

G. P. Putnam's Sons

G. P. PUTNAM'S SONS
An imprint of Penguin Random House LLC
1745 Broadway, New York, New York 10019

First published in the United States of America by G. P. Putnam's Sons,
an imprint of Penguin Random House LLC, 2025

Copyright © 2025 by Arriel Vinson

Penguin Random House values and supports copyright. Copyright fuels creativity, encourages diverse voices, promotes free speech, and creates a vibrant culture. Thank you for buying an authorized edition of this book and for complying with copyright laws by not reproducing, scanning, or distributing any part of it in any form without permission. You are supporting writers and allowing Penguin Random House to continue to publish books for every reader. Please note that no part of this book may be used or reproduced in any manner for the purpose of training artificial intelligence technologies or systems.

G. P. Putnam's Sons is a registered trademark of Penguin Random House LLC. The Penguin colophon is a registered trademark of Penguin Books Limited.

Visit us online at PenguinRandomHouse.com.

Library of Congress Cataloging-in-Publication Data is available.

ISBN 9780593858592

10 9 8 7 6 5 4 3 2 1

Manufactured in the United States of America

BVG

Design by Alex Campbell
Text set in Celeste Pro

This book is a work of fiction. Any references to historical events, real people, or real places are used fictitiously. Other names, characters, places, and events are products of the author's imagination, and any resemblance to actual events or places or persons, living or dead, is entirely coincidental.

The publisher does not have any control over and does not assume any responsibility for author or third-party websites or their content.

The authorized representative in the EU for product safety and compliance is Penguin Random House Ireland, Morrison Chambers, 32 Nassau Street, Dublin D02 YH68, Ireland, https://eu-contact.penguin.ie.

We hang on to our no place
happy to be alive
—Lucille Clifton

For my family,
who taught me
to be loud.

For the Black girls
who are still
figuring out how to be.

One

School just ended
and the sticky summer humidity
brings us to WestSide Roll,
only a five-minute drive from home.

The skating rink is our place
every Saturday night.

Me, my bestie Noelle, every skater here
whip around the wood, fast and furious
like we're racing for our lives.

We shake our sorrows loose,
shed them like snakeskin.

We're too loud   young   Black
for other places in Indianapolis,

so we're here,
where neon lights tint lockers and white tees,
brighten the confetti-print carpet.

We roll around as our toes go numb,
as our calves throb from dancing
and bending to the beat.

Sometimes we get into shit.
Sometimes we fall in love.
Sometimes we fall out.

But none of that stops us
from losing ourselves on the slick floor
till all the lights come up,
till our parents text us
to get our asses in the car.

I slide onto the skate floor with the flow of traffic,
weaving in and out of the thick crowd to avoid collision.
Noelle skates by my side, fanning herself with her hand.

The buttery scent of popcorn and nacho cheese
mixed with socks and sweat fills the rink.

DJ Sunny, an oldhead, is in his booth
in the middle of the rink floor,
spinning a rap song that he plays every Saturday night.

Bouncing as I skate,
my feet follow the beat,
wheels slapping the maple.

I love spotting the skate crews
Naptown Rollers, NapSk8z, WestSide Riders
in their matching tees,

skate names on the back,
social handles underneath,
carefully laid out like an infographic.

Ron, the cameraman, records to post later,
showcasing our skills for skaters from other cities
to convene in the comments.

Noe and I pass couples backpacking,
pass girls our age, sixteen and stumbling,

like it's the first time their feet have donned
the tan suede rental skates.
Pass the regulars:

Mook and Lailani, *the* couple of NapSk8z crew.
Tiana, the best skater my age, who doesn't miss a Saturday night.
Tiana's mama, Julia. A WestSide Riders member who could be
   co-owner with how often she's here.
Mr. Kareem, an oldhead who teaches us smoother ways to
        glide   float   soar.
Miss Charlene, a Naptown Roller with the longest nails, wildest
   footwork, and best burgers at Steak 'n Shake Monday through
   Wednesday.

Some of them know me from when
I've jumped into their routine
trying to learn something different
from what my parents taught me.

No purses or bags while skating, y'all,
DJ Sunny announces over the mic.

The song he spins makes me want to fly.
I leave Noe for a second
'cause she doesn't skate as fast as me,
our skate styles as different as we are.

                Where her movements
                      are quiet,
            a gentle sway or subtle snap,

mine are intricate,
arms out, reaching for something
bigger than me,
footwork too complex to copy.

Outside of the skate floor,
I'm the quiet one.

                              Outside of the skate floor,
                                        Noe shines.
                  She tries new things, flirts with a crush,
                attempts to drag me to unfamiliar places
                                and almost always,
                                          I tell her
                                  I'd rather stay in
                              with my soothing R&B.

I'm gonna link with Kaila and Ashley,
Noe says before skating off.
I don't get to ask where
or if I should come along.

I watch her sway
past the glittering disco balls,
the metallic fringe streamers
hanging from the ceiling,
the neon lights shining green
on her light skin
until she's off the rink floor
and onto the carpet, blending with the crowd.

It's been this way since she made the dance team.
Her kinda detached.
Me kinda alone.

DJ Sunny gets on the mic
with recycled lines I savor.

How y'all feeling tonight?

The lights flicker on above the rink floor,
remove us from the shadows.

We gonna get it rockin'.
Remember, if you don't have skates on,
you cannot *be on the rink floor.*
If you wanna dance, go by the lockers.
If you don't wanna turn up at WestSide Roll, go home.

We shout the last bit with him,
echoing the mantra that makes us family.

As much as I love skating with Noe
shoulder to shoulder
while we scope out cute guys,

I also love skating alone.

Just me. Eyes closed,
(little) hips swinging,
mouth   wide, singing loudly.

Even though the rink
is always noisy—skaters shouting, singing,
counting for a routine,
jumping into a spin—
in your zone, you can't hear none of it.

So here I am in the middle of the skate floor
hoping to sweat out everything I've pent up inside.

I spin to a mid-tempo song
I can get lost in,
wrap myself around each note
like a weighted blanket.

My father taught me this
before he became someone
I could no longer love loudly.

I spread my arms wide
then bring them close for balance

he taught me how to close myself off
from love

spin

        spin

                spin

I am a tornado
tearing through the rink
I throw my arms   back   out
sharp and straight
doing a 360 spin

He taught me how to turn away quickly,

how to avoid
being still

being stuck

staying.

As my feet   glide across
the sleek floor,

I close my eyes,
hum the melody,

        let it take over.
        let it take over.
        let it take over.

Then a body

                        slams

                        into me,

                        knocks

                        me

                        down.

I'm writhing,
trying to get up,
and that's the hardest part
about falling in the first place.

The first rule of WestSide Roll:

Watch where you're going.

I look up, try to focus
on the culprit
who lets *sorry*
spill from his mouth
again and again
like it's the only word he knows.

He towers over me,
smooth brown skin glistening with sweat,
thick eyebrows in such panic
that they nearly meet his coily hairline.

> I say, *It's okay*,
> and his shoulders relax.

He's gorgeous so I forgive
the mistake despite the pain
shooting through my back.

He stares
and I imagine he's studying
all the parts of me I try not to think about.

My curly strands now astray
my ordinary brown eyes
my wide nose and plump cheeks
my skinny frame
my deep-brown skin.

My parents met at WestSide Roll.

My mama would chase

my dad on skates,

steal his sweat towel

from his back pocket

(which is gross, really)

and hope he'd catch her.

He did, and I never asked for the rest

of the story but I know

they were here every weekend,

tall tees to their knees,

baby hair gel-slicked and swooped,

chunky gold rope chains

against their chests like Olympic medals.

I've seen pictures

and couldn't help

but laugh at the fashions.

Don't be laughin',

we were fly,

my mama would say,

tucking the photos

back into her album.

I take it you don't skate often, I say.

The guy rubs his palm over his curly
hair, faded sides, down to his neck,
then looks into my eyes.

He sticks out the same hand to help me up
and says, *I'm new here.*

Which is obvious.

Newcomers keep their eyes locked on
other skaters' synchronized feet,
stunned by our quickness.

Once I'm up, I do what's expected of me,
tell him my name is Jaelyn,
but he can call me Jae.

Wassup, JJ. I'm Trey.

He reaches his hand out again, and I'm not confident
I can handle his petal-soft touch a second time.

He doesn't drop his gaze.
A slight smile inches across his face.

I meet his hand,
my fingers trembling.

I said Jae.

I know.

I roll my eyes, let go,
already knowing
he's way too sure of himself.

I skate off and exit the rink floor, leaving him behind.

He's one of those guys
who turns heads when he skates by.

One of those guys that a girl would
drop everything for.

So beautiful that even
the prettiest might doubt herself.

He's probably self-centered,
maybe an athlete,
always keeps a girlfriend.

I don't have the space to think about him.

Not today, not tomorrow, not any day.

My problems   take up   all the room.

I have to tell Noe what happened

but I can barely squeeze through

the dancing crowd near the lockers,

girls squatting low like they got Megan Thee Stallion knees.

I push between bodies,

trying to avoid new Dunks and sandaled feet,

my skates on carpet slowing my efforts.

I spot Noe with Kaila and Ashley

laughing so hard you can see their teeth,

white bright like polished porcelain.

They lean into each other, share a secret,

eyes darting like people can hear them over the music.

I finally reach them and the whispers stop.

They stand side by side, a wall that can't be knocked down.

Kaila and Ashley give me slight smiles and waves,

Noe frowns.

Icees? I shout, pointing to the concession stand.

Right now? she asks, but doesn't budge.

Our routine goes like this:

skate together, skate apart,

dance near the lockers,

get Icees from the Roller Café,

go home.

Just grab me my favorite,
she finally says.

I nod but my heart
                      falls
hangs suspended in the sharp air between us
and I think it might crash and shatter.

I skate toward the Roller Café,
beg my skates to cooperate on the carpet.

The minute I get in line,
my mama texts our group chat
that she's pulling up in three minutes,
So be ready.

As I walk to the exit, my skates are tucked into my side
like you'd hold a newborn. I wrap my hand around the toe
of my left skate, hide the peeling material.

For the most part, we regulars treat our skates
like precious cargo. Clean, shine, buff
to keep them in the same condition we bought them in.
But I've learned in these, lived in these.

A new pair means me or my mama cut into a bill.

Once the suffocating outdoor air reaches my skin,
I see my mama parked at the curb,
blinkers on, windows down.

Somehow, Noe is already in the front seat.

> *Dang, eager,* I mumble,
> then open the back door
> and shuffle inside.

You snooze, you lose.

My mama asks the usual:

How was the rink?
Were a lot of people there?
Any fights?
Any cute boys? (I never answer that one.)
Did y'all have fun?

I want to respond:

We were sweat against sweat,
voice over voice.

Still, it was lonely.

No Noelle by my side most of the night.

I met a guy and I keep replaying
the moment in my head.

I felt freest when my feet were gliding.
When I stood still
I had too much time to think.

My mama and Noe chat away, finish each other's sentences
like *they're* the mother and daughter

I let my window down
invite the warm breeze in

stare at our ever-changing neighborhood

the luxury apartment signs sprouting like weeds

the gourmet cupcake shop that used to be a record store

the Black-owned beauty supply store now an art gallery

the payday loan place replaced by a flower shop

the empty unit next to it promoting a Blow Dry Bar coming soon

the barbershop next to that still standing

the Dairy Queen that's been here for decades still full of people

the same yellowing grass lining the sidewalks
on either side of High School Road
still begging for care

When me and my mama moved to the West Side
after the divorce, I thought I'd never get used to it.

It took a year, maybe two, but now I expect the water gun fights
between Ezekiel and Jr. (no one knows his real name)
that I sometimes get caught in the crossfire of

and the late-night pickup games
with the raggedy hoop that stands at the end of the building,
net dangling from the rim like an earring

and bass bumping from hellcats
that drive by with the windows down

and the way we dance
to music spilling from apartments,
flooding the sidewalks.

The noise would swallow my old suburb whole.
Plainfield, Indiana, was:

quiet,
only loud when children exited school buses,
backpacks slapping as they ran;

spacious,
the yards stretched far and wide,
gave us room to breathe;

abundant,

stores fully stocked,

products displayed like precious stones;

mostly white,

it was rare to see people like us

hair kinked, loc'd, or silked.

To hear anyone speaking like we speak.

The three of us file into my apartment,

drop our skates at the door,

latch the bottom lock,

then the top, and add the security bar.

My mama plops a good night kiss

on each of our foreheads.

I wipe the leftover wetness

as she disappears to her room.

Me and Noe go to mine,

toss our belongings all over

my bedroom floor

    scattered   like spilled   grains of rice.

We used to talk until 3 or 4 a.m.

about her newest crush

or moments from last semester

or dreams of how our junior year will go.

But tonight, she's quiet

I'm quiet

and no one

breaks

This happens often now.

Each time, the silences are longer.
What used to be one revolution
around the rink

is now a few songs at the rink long.

Noe and I became best friends in sixth grade
when I moved from Plainfield, thirty minutes away from here.

We shared all of our classes.
She wouldn't stop asking,
What's the homework?
Do you have a pen?

Finally
she passed me a pink notebook,
the first page half full with frilly handwriting,
hearts dotting the *i*'s,
formally introducing herself
and complaining about Mrs. Greenwalder.

We talked about everything
in those pages.
Our days,
the boys we liked,
the clothes we wanted,
our weekend plans.

Back then, we were both lonely.
My parents were divorced.
Hers had run off.

When she invited me over
for the first time, months
into the semester, she said,
I live with my grandma.

A warning. A confession.

When I invited her over for the first time,
I said, *I live with just my mama.*
An equal trade. My truth for hers.

The next morning,

we all walk to Noe's granny's apartment,
only two buildings over in the same complex.

Mrs. Joyce, who I call Granny
'cause she's like my own,
comes to the screen door,
her light-brown skin cloaked in
a purple robe, short gray hair in a purple bonnet.

>   *Hey, Granny!*
>   I say as I open the door
>   so Noe can bring her stuff in.

Good morning, y'all, she says.

We go in,
remove our shoes at the door,
careful not to disturb the freshly vacuumed carpet,

make ourselves comfortable
on the plastic-covered couch
that crunches when we sit.

How was the rink?
Granny asks.

Noe and I repeat the spiel we gave my mama.

After, me and Noe don't even glance at each other.

My mama and Granny discuss the news.

Noe starts texting,

the smiling and laughing return.

Later that day, me and my mama
head to the laundromat by our apartment.

The one about a three-minute drive from us.

We haul our identical hampers in,
find two working machines side by side,
load our clothes extra quick
as if it'll get us out of here faster.

Our washer at home is out of commission.
Again.

The washers wear a layer of dirt,
some of them leak, water snaking
between our shoes,
half of the dryers are down.

I'm at one washer and she's at another,
barely speaking, only sorting.

A man walks up to us,
Aye, I got perfumes and oils the ladies love.
One for $10 or two for $18.

No thanks, my mama says without looking.

She slams her washer shut,
jams the quarters inside.

We settle into the black banquet chairs—
vinyl splitting at the seams,

cotton inside escaping
like I want to.

I never want to see this place again
but our neighborhood has been overrun
by new stores
new residents
new problems

and this broken-down laundromat is almost all we have left.

Two

It's always hectic at the theater on $5 Tuesdays.

I'm working the box office this evening,
which, here, is just a register stationed in the corner of the lobby.

I ring up family after family
for the newest animated movie.

I want to hush all the crying
and screaming bouncing off the walls.

I check my phone.
Two and a half hours left

with my hovering,
too-many-tasks-assigning pest of a manager, Beth.

A group of girls enters

that I can hear but not see yet,
laughing from their bellies.

They round the corner and it's only three people:
Kaila, Ashley, and a surprisingly empty-handed Noe.

She usually brings me food during my fifteen
that I scarf down because this theater only offers
basic concessions: popcorn, nachos, Icees.

Heyyy, Jae, Noe sings,
Kaila and Ashley behind her,
beaming bright as the marquee out front.

> *Hey, girl,* I say, clipped.
> *Are you seeing a movie?*

How's work? she asks,
leans her elbows on the galaxy granite counter.

> *Loud and annoying.*

I don't see how you do it,
Kaila adds, scanning the theater
like she's never been before.

I want to say,
I don't have a choice.
This is the place that hired me.

Me neither, I say instead, and turn my attention back to Noe.

We're having team time today, here . . . Noe trails off.
To see Don't Fall in Love with Me.

Well, I wish you could have waited for me,
I say.

I log back into my timed-out screen
as she tells me how excited she is
about the newest Black romance
that I was saving to watch with her.

We fell in love with rom-coms freshman year
and once I started working here,
we ran my discount up,

used it every Friday night that I wasn't scheduled,
took mental notes of what we should look for
when we get a romance of our own:

flowers—preferably a bouquet of roses
a curated playlist—preferably songs with a grand message
impromptu dates—preferably on our worst days
genuine confessions of love—preferably forever.

I plop the Be Back Soon sign down
on the counter and join them
as they order two of everything
from my co-worker behind concessions, Connor.

Me and Noe chow down
on a large bucket of popcorn,
Kaila and Ashley laugh again.

A hot heaviness looms behind me.

Beth.

Jaelyn, can you all quiet down?
You're disturbing our moviegoers.

She pronounces my name *Jah-lyn*
instead of *Jay-lyn.*
Like it hurts a little.
Like she's searching for something in her mouth.
Like my mother spelled it wrong.

I scan the room for the moviegoers in question.

> *There isn't anyone out here now,*
> *and we're not that loud,* I say.

We're eye to eye.
I examine her crow's feet,
her furrowed brows,

her blue eyes,

cold and crystal like a glacier.

You are *being loud. I don't want to escalate this conflict.*

My tongue is hot

with a comeback

but I fail

to find

my words.

I walk into Steak 'n Shake after work
for some alone time
and am greeted by Miss Charlene.

How you doin', Jaelyn?
She points me to my booth
with red acrylic nails so long they curve.

The half-price milkshake happy hour
crowd has thinned out,
leaving most seats empty.

Whole order?
Miss Charlene shouts
over the hissing oil from the fryer.

She is often cook / host /
server / drive-thru expert
because this location is notoriously understaffed.

    Yep, whole thing, I shout back
    as I wiggle into a comfortable position.

I always sit by myself, download a show
on my phone, decompress.

A laugh fills up the room, then
All right, bro, I'll hit you up later.

The voice sparks a fire in me.

Trey from the rink heads right toward me,
his brown eyes staring into mine.

Hey, JJ, he says, then snatches his AirPods out.

I break contact, stare down at the empty table
as my heart starts beating triple time.
And a yearning I never asked for alights.

He slides into my booth opposite me,
smile spreading like warm butter,
dimples exposing themselves.

I've never considered how awkward I look
dining by myself, sticking out like a cherry stem in a vanilla shake.

Can I sit here?

Strike one: He's not a great skater.

Strike two: He doesn't know how to leave people alone.

But I don't mind his attention.

> *You've already sat down,*
> I say, and quirk a brow.

He doesn't stop smiling, only leans in
like he has gossip to share.

I saw you and thought
you might want company.

> *My boyfriend is on his way.*

Oh shit. My bad.

He starts to get up.

> *I'm joking,* I say,
> smiling but holding in my laugh.

He sinks back down.

So I'm dealing with the next big stand-up comedian? Got it.

Miss Charlene sashays over,
smirks at me, asks Trey what he'd like.

He was loud when he walked in,
but for a moment, he's silent,

R&B music and sizzling steak burgers
the only sounds.

He finally orders.

When she leaves, he focuses in on me
like he didn't see me well in the darkness of WestSide Roll.

Maybe he didn't.

Maybe, up close, I'm not what he thought.

*I didn't think you could get more beautiful
than you were the other night*, he says.

My eyes grow twice their size
and his fist flies
to his mouth

covers his lips
like forbidden information
just escaped them.

I look everywhere but him
and say, *Oh, thank you.*

What I see of him now under the fluorescent lights:

Brown eyes with an ocean water sparkle

Dimples deep enough to drown in

Coily hair moisturized like it was just dipped in oil

Shoulders wide and square

A smile responsible for stealing the air from my lungs

Miss Charlene brings out my shake—
half-strawberry, half-banana—
and leaves two straws on the table with a wink.

Trey and I lock eyes.
A choice sits between us.

Noe would tell me to share with the cute guy.
Move to his side of the booth, get close.

But all of that would mean something
and I don't need anything to mean anything right now.

> I'll ask Miss Charlene for a second shake.
> She extends happy hour for me.

His chest deflates.
But he catches himself and perks back up,
smile reappearing as if I've said something funny.

There was this move you did
at the rink the other night. I liked it.

> *You were watching me?*

Before now, I never
wondered if other people
observed me while I skate.

In my mind, I'm a graceful swan
gliding across the skate floor,

neck and back arching with each movement,
but there are no mirrors in a rink

so who knows if I look as fluid
as I feel when I'm out there.

Yeah, I was.
You knocked into me
and shook my brain up a little.
I could only see you after that.

> *Boy, please, you knocked into* me, I say, and laugh.
> *What was the move?*

Trey stands up.

I make sure the older man a few booths away
is still glued to the book he's reading.

It was something like this,
Trey says,
then kicks,
slides forward so he's at the next booth,
bends each knee one by one,
and ends with a bounce and clap.

He's about to start again
but I'm in the booth cracking up,
hand clutching my stomach
like it'll force the laughter
back into my body.

~ 42 ~

Damn, I look funny?

He settles back into his seat,
joins me in laughing until we're so loud,
Miss Charlene peeks her head from the kitchen and shouts,

Y'all good over there?

> *We're good.*
> Our voices meld together
> like instruments in a song.

Finally, we wind down,
catch each other's eyes.

I can tell by the look of him

by the way my stomach flutters at his low-pitched voice

by the way I am cotton candy dissolving the minute he cracks a joke

that I need to safeguard my heart.

Miss Charlene presents his shake,
vanilla with M&M's, and he eats
a big spoonful, then another.

How did you learn to skate?
He asks after a mouthful.

My parents taught me.

Can you teach me?

I pause, remember his two left feet,
the way I could have broken
a limb because of him.

Why do you wanna learn?

His turn to pause.
He looks past the booths across from us
and out the window.

My parents said I need to find a safe hobby
or they're done with me.

I don't ask the questions bouncing in my head:
what his definition of safe is
because skating without gear is dangerous,
what would make parents be done
with their son at his age.

Then again,
I'm done with my dad.

*There are plenty of other skaters
to choose from.*

He brushes his hand over his curls,
chews on his lip.

But you've been alone the two times I've seen you.

                I thought I was the only one
                who noticed my loneliness.

You're alone, too.

Miss Charlene sets our food
on the table, steam rising like fog.

>*What do I get for teaching you?* I ask.

He playfully places his hands
on his chest, one over the other.
I can offer you my loyal, undying,
super-funny friendship.

>*When does the funny start?*

Don't play like you ain't been
laughing this whole time.

He throws a fry at me and I catch it.

Shake on it? he asks,
extending the offending hand,
nails so clean they look manicured.

My hand meets his, and I ignore
the electric current running
through our fingers.

Do you need a ride home?

Trey asks as we make our way outside.

> *Bye, Miss Charlene.*
> *See you at the rink tomorrow!*
> I shout over my shoulder.

She throws a wave my direction.

Trey opens the door for me,
stands beside it with his hand out
like a church usher
to welcome me into the heat.

> *No, that's okay.*
> *I'm gonna call an Uber.*

He throws his hands up in surrender.

Tell me I've been bad company
without telling me I've been bad company.

He leans against the white
painted brick wall, props his foot up.
I stand in front of him,
arms locked behind my back.

He's staring again.

I hope my skin is radiant
because I surely neglected moisturizer this morning.

I hope my curly hair isn't frizzy from the heat
and each strand falls in its rightful place.

I hope my smile isn't taking up my whole face
squeezing my eyes small.

> *You could be a weirdo,*
> I say to distract him from staring.

*And you're gonna teach
a weirdo how to skate?*

> *Mm, good point.*
> *Maybe I shouldn't.*

*Let's not go there! Let me show you
your possible Uber for the evening.
I'll be okay with whatever choice
you make, but a little heartbroken
if you don't choose Betsy.*

He walks across the lot
and I follow, shaking my head
behind his easy stride.

> *Who is Betsy?*
> I ask.

Her.

We stop in front of a matte black Dodge Challenger,
the tinted windows almost as dark as the tires.

I know those tints are illegal.

Just below the illegal limit.

He puts on a car salesman voice,
chipper and quick, marches around the car.

Here we have Betsy, a 2023 Dodge Challenger.
She can get up to 203 miles per hour,
but that's strictly forbidden.
She likes sunsets, loud music,
and quiet moments at the lake.
Her tank costs about $70.

He arrives at the hood of the car.
But you ride free of charge.

My cheeks are hot like a stovetop,
enough to yank my hand away from the surface.

    Free, you say?
    I jump into character with him.

Zero dollars and zero cents. Every ride.

    How do you profit?

I get your time. I think that's good enough.
Even though you could be a weirdo.

    I could be.

He shrugs.

I guess we'll have to see.

The only requirement is your number—

you know, in case you leave anything.

He hands me his phone,

bulkier than mine,

too big for my hands.

I save my contact as Jaelyn 🛼 ☺

Our fingertips meet

when I return it,

the soft brush sending tingles

down my spine.

Your chariot awaits,

he says, opening the passenger door.

I sink into the seat,

stick my hands under my thighs

to keep them from burning against the grill-hot leather.

As Trey pulls out of the lot,

alternative R&B slinks through speakers

and he shimmies, snaps, before any lyrics begin,

looks at me expectantly like I should join.

    You look ridiculous, I say.

He almost has rhythm,
shoulders moving a second after
the beat itself,

but it's adorable.

*I was listening to this before
I got to Steak 'n Shake,*
he says. *Song of the summer.*

Things I learn about Trey as he drives well below the speed limit:

- He talks a lot.
- About everything.
- His laugh sounds like an engine failing to start.
- His eyes dance when he's listening.
- He asks more questions than an interrogator.
    - While sidestepping half of mine.
        - He doesn't talk about where he moved from or tell me why.
- He says he doesn't like to brag.
    - But he does.
    - Constantly.
    - About how much he benches.
    - And how well he thinks he can sing (it's not accurate).
    - And rap.
    - And somehow it's not annoying.
- He breaks out in song randomly.
- He lightens the mood.
- He's even cuter with the sun beaming on him.

As we approach my porch
I hear, but don't see, Ezekiel and Jr.
Oooo, Jaelyn, who is that?
as if Trey isn't right here.

Noe is the only person I bring around.

Up here, Jr. shouts
from the nook of a tree
all twisted up like a breakdancer,
trying to keep his body steady.

    Y'all are so nosy! Where is your mama?

At wooooork, they say in unison.

They leap from the tree,
run to meet us
as we get to my step.

Ezekiel sticks his hand out,
I'm Ezekiel. You can call me Zeek.

I raise an eyebrow.
No one calls him that.
Trey leans down and shakes up with him.

Nice to meet you, Zeek. I'm Trey.

I'm Jr. Are you Jaelyn's boyfriend?

Jr. doesn't bother shaking hands.

Um, no. We just met. She's my skate coach.

Mhm, that's what they all say,
Ezekiel says.

> *Y'all, let us have a moment*
> *before I tell y'all mama*
> *that you were bothering strangers!*

They scurry off,
little legs carrying them far
down the sidewalk
and into another tree.

We stand face-to-face,
taking each other in.

Trey stares at me intently.

> *I feel like you're trying to figure me out.*

Something like that.

> *Can't you just ask me what you want to know?*

I want to know everything.

I'm learning he leads with curiosity.
I lead with silence.
Observing more than I speak.

Wondering more than I ask.
Learning more than I share.

I look away, tuck my smile.
He inches closer.

So close
I smell the milkshake on his breath,
his cologne, citrus and woody,
an invitation to a place far away from here.

> *I had a good time*, I say,
> almost backing
> into the screen door.

Me too, he says.
He opens his arms
for a hug and I let him embrace me,
stay in his arms like I've always known them.

I flop onto my bed and FaceTime Noe,
feet on the postered wall of my favorite singers.
Beyoncé. SZA. Ari Lennox. Jill Scott. Jazmine Sullivan.

The women who ground me
when I don't have my footing.
My fairy lights make them glow.

Noe answers in the dark,
her bullet journals stacked on the bookcase
behind her, along with magazines of the rich Black women
she dreams of being.

> *Girl, not Trey wanting me to teach him how to skate.*
> *We never start with hellos,*
> *get right into it.*

Who is Trey?

I forgot I never told her.
I find his social media
as fast as I can, screenshot, and share.

> *I ran into him at the rink. Well, he ran into me.*
> *He saw me at Steak 'n Shake tonight*
> *and sat with me, then asked if I would teach him.*

She sits up.
Wellllllll?

> *I think I should?*

Duh, you should.

Noe cheeses like she dreamed of this moment.

So when's the first lesson?

> *Thursday, during Soul Night,* I say.

Only two days to prepare?

> My turn to sit up.
> *He chose this week!*
> *I wasn't thinking!*
> *I was overwhelmed.*

So he's running things?

> *Noe, please. Just tell me what I'm supposed to do.*
> *He's so cute but I don't want anything right now.*

Why not?

I tell her I just started reading
all these books about
self-love
self-worth
and not seeking relationships
until you've done the work.

I mean, we're not twenty-eight. We're . . . sixteen.

> *I am almost seventeen,* I say. *That's almost twenty-one!*

If you think healing is best, do that.
But he seems cool, don't be weird.

    Who said anything about being weird?

Noe sighs.
I know you. You're gonna teach him
and then be all awkward so you don't start liking him.

    Noe, just tell me what to wear.
    Say.
    Do.

Okay, hold on. My teammate Asha
is calling, let me call you right back.

    Noe, really?

Yes! I'll call you right back.

        I wait
        and wait,
        checking my phone
        every so often,

        jumping at every vibration,
        assuming it's her
        each time my screen lights up.

        But she never calls.

Three

Soul Night on Thursdays

is never as packed as Saturdays.
The crowd is different: diehards only.

I hurry past the skate rental,
happy to ignore the musty skates I wore as a kid,
orange toe stops scuffed, laces frayed.

Mr. Mike, the owner, does crazy legs on the rink floor,
wiggling one leg in front of the other,
harder than it sounds but a sort of magic.

I find a seat to lace my skates up.
Left foot first, sliding the white boot
over my ankle, tugging it secure.

I pull my hot pink laces tight,
lace them all the way up the tongue,
leaving some shoestring to loop around the top
and tie in the front.

More important than how you look is the look of your skates.
Some skaters spend a check or two to create their own:
heels or Converse on top of wheels,
shearling lining, custom colors, anything to be different.

I glide onto the rink floor

and immediately fall into rhythm,

wheels rolling against the wood

like a bowling ball aiming for a strike.

Soul Night is for the funk/electronic,

R&B, and neo-soul lovers.

The crowd is mostly older folks,

me and a few other young skaters in the minority.

I catch the tempo of a smooth nineties song,

let the girl group trio take me away,

sing along,

lift my arms in the air like I can grab onto the ceiling.

Trey inches around
the inner rink,
where the slower skaters are.

My stomach grows wings
flutters
my feet slow
my legs lose the beat.

Skaters fly by
trying new stunts
but all I can see
is him.

I get near.

> *You're learning,*
> I yell over the music.

His legs start to give and he grabs my arm.
I almost slip.

Dang, you almost made me fall,
he says, and straightens.

> *How did I do that?* I ask, regaining balance.

You make me nervous,
he says, eyes stuck on his rental skates
like they'll walk off on their own.

The twinkle in Trey's eyes
and the soft twitch of his lips
make me want to toss
my fears in the trash.

> I ignore his comment.
> *How about the basics today?*

Do I have to learn?

> *I didn't realize you were a quitter.*

We pass skaters in the middle, learning, too,
falling, getting up, grabbing onto each other.
Suddenly, I notice
all the touching that I didn't account for.

*Naw, I don't quit. It just looks
easier than it is.*

> *Everything isn't as easy as it appears,*
> I reply.

Okay, Socrates.

> *Whatever.* I laugh and roll my eyes.
> *Let's work on balance and speed.*

I pick up my pace,
smiling over my shoulder at his unsure legs.

The minute he quickens,
he falls, stretched out on the floor.
Necks crane to make sure he's okay.

Once I realize he's good,
my laugh overpowers the music,
tears flow down my face.

Relax on me. Relax,
he says from the ground.
I stick my hand out,
waiting for him to take it.

He clutches my hand tight
and I lead him to a bench.

Are you gonna try again?
I ask.

I need an Icee to cure my embarrassment.

His body hunches over. He rests
his hand on his head, faking a faint,
dimples appearing each time
his wide grin shows itself.

My smile
appears without permission.

How am I supposed to teach you
if you keep giving up?

He replies in his fake faint.
I never said I'd be easy to teach.

DJ Sunny announces slow-skate,

and R&B turns the whole rink
molasses slow. Sticky sweat
cooled by the ebb and flow
of the oldhead lovers breezing by.

The lights dim and some skaters leave the floor.
Others spin around to skate backward.

This is the quietest time at WestSide Roll,
a few snaps, some singing,

but mostly we're close to someone else
or wondering what close would feel like.

Every skater here knows
the song by the intro notes alone.

> *I'm gonna skate to this before we go,*
> I say to Trey, smoothing my clothes out.

I wanna skate, too.

> *I thought you gave up?*
> I ask.

I can hold on to you though, right?

The butterflies in my stomach / tell me to run / I respond to Trey / *maybe next time* / watch him flatten / feel the butterflies flap away / I can't / start something with him / when everything / I used to believe / about love / that it's forever / that it's worth / my whole heart / has been disproven / when every time I think / about trying / I remember / anyone can leave me / if my own father can.

Before it gets awkward,

I rush to skate alone.

As much as I want Trey,
it's easier to stay friendly.

I feel his eyes as I spin to backward skate
to Tevin Campbell's "Can We Talk,"
a WestSide Roll classic
that usually puts me at ease.

But today I'm completely off beat,
moving two times the speed
of other skaters.

My hands sweat,
my stomach is in knots,
body so tense even a masseuse couldn't loosen it.

I slow down.

I hum,
briefly close my eyes,
inhale deep,
exhale through the mouth,
and there it is.

The feeling of freedom.

A brief history:

My parents taught me how to backward skate.

My dad was the better teacher.
I still remember his words:
knees bent, one foot in front, then the other.

My mama only said, *Just feel it.*

The music lowers,

bright lights shine again,

no more darkness

to hide in.

WestSide Roll has been amazing, DJ Sunny starts.

We all slow down even more,

gather toward the DJ booth,

trade confused glances.

DJ Sunny is so close to the mic / he could kiss it / he recalls skate memories / asking us to remember with him / some skaters glance at each other / remember together

We love the magic / WestSide Roll's ability to make a good day out of a bad one / We love the community / the same guaranteed skaters / every Thursday / Saturday / no matter what / no matter how long it takes for some to drive here / We love that it's the constant / in our lives / sometimes the only thing / keeping us / stress-free / or out of trouble

No matter our age / at WestSide Roll / we come together / share / unleash / be everything we have to apologize for elsewhere

He hands the mic to Mr. Mike,
who looks out like he wants
to capture us standing side by side.

We are clumped in clusters,
Naptown Rollers, NapSk8z,
and WestSide Riders standing together,
Mr. Kareem and Mook at the edges,
still rolling around a bit.

Any time I see Mr. Mike
he's in motion,
whether it's checking on the café
or running skate rental because someone
called out of work

or flowing on the wood,
trying something new,
or joining a skate line.

This is the first time
that I've seen him

                          still.

He looks tired,

eyes baggy, body slouched,

beard rugged.

WestSide Roll has been my baby for decades, he finally says.

My place to get the community together,

get young folk off the street, old folk out a funk.

He rubs his bald head, ceiling lights making it shinier.

The pit of my stomach makes itself known.

I tap my toe stop against the wood,

feet nervous as my insides.

It's been a good run, y'all, but I'm sorry to say that

WestSide Roll is closing in five weeks.

It's like someone
snatched the breath
out of my body
I don't see anything
only hear *aw man*'s
or *what the fuck*'s
I am motionless
wondering how
something so special
to me
to us
could disappear

Trey has to force me
off the rink floor, playing
tug of war with my arms.

>*I can't believe it*, I say.

He rubs my back like he's calming a baby.

Everyone starts to exit,
shoulders slumped,
tension a tightrope.

As we leave the building,
I grab my phone
and find my text thread
with my mama to tell her the news.

Do you want to talk about it?
Trey asks.

>*No.*

Okay. Do you want me to take you home?

>*I was going to take the bus.*

I can take you home. If you want, I mean.

>*Thank you. The bus is fine. I need to be alone.*

Let me at least drive you to the stop.

Pull up right here,

    I say once he gets close,
    and I reach for the car door handle.

The bus stop is on a side street
around the corner from the rink,
ducked off from the busyness.

Don't you want to wait until
you see the bus coming?

    How will the driver see me?
    I ask.

My bad, my bad.

No one else is here yet,
still hanging in the parking lot
processing the news together.
I needed to get away.

I get out of the car and Trey rolls
the passenger window down.

I'm staying until the bus comes, though,
he says.

    Now you're my parent?

No, I told you I'd be your friend.
Undying loyalty and bus watches included.

Trey gets out and joins me at the stop,
rolls up his sleeves
to expose his smooth biceps.

We talk about what it felt like
for him to skate, how free I looked
when he watched me.

How before he moved, he didn't
have hobbies that he shared with others,
didn't participate in school stuff.

How in Carmel, Indiana,
a suburb forty minutes north of where we are now,
public transportation barely existed.

How, in Carmel, he did a lot of pretending.
As he talks, he uses his house key to softly
carve shapes into his palm.

Before I can ask what he means,
the bus arrives and I move to the curb.

Trey follows, his arm slightly
brushing against mine.
A shiver moves through me.

I'm sorry the rink is closing,
he says, and gazes into my eyes.

I can only nod,
manage a *thank you.*

I scroll through

my WestSide Roll album
on the way home.

I have photos of me and Noe
our first time there together,
stale silk presses and huge smiles,
our rental skates like clown shoes.

Videos of Mr. Mike
teaching the Naptown Rollers
how to snake walk, slithering one leg
while keeping the other rolling.

DJ Sunny in his bag,
mixing soul with funk with trap with R&B
until everybody's skating so fast
they sweat.

Finally, I reach
a picture of our once family.
My father with his infamous sweat rag.
My mama showing off almost every body part.
Me in the middle
with a peace sign,
glowing.

My chest is full of something heavy
and a call comes in, "Father" at the top of the screen.

His timing is always the worst.
I hit decline before it fully rings.

Not even a minute later,
he texts me.

Hey baby girl.
I heard about the rink . . . Are you okay?
I want to see you . . . Maybe we can skate together again.
My knees aren't what they used to be . . . but I still got it.
What do you think? 🙏

I bring my legs close,
curl into a ball,
stare out the window
until my stop.

A brief history:

Before their divorce was final,
my mama got on the phone
with my auntie one day

and I glued my ear
to the popcorned white wall
as she whispered,

He agreed so fast,
and I just want to know how long
he's been wanting to leave,
how long the loss of our baby
meant the loss of my husband, too.

She never used
the word *miscarriage*.
Just *loss. Loss. Loss.*

It's been four years since he left
three since we stopped talking daily
two since he forgot my birthday
one since we've spent time together

but I'm still foolishly hoping
that he'll return to the fun-loving
father he used to be.

Four

TWENTY-SIX DAYS UNTIL WESTSIDE ROLL CLOSES

I've been in my room all day, doomscrolling.

Outside my window Ezekiel, Jr., and other neighborhood kids
scream and throw balls against brick.

My mama is in the kitchen, pots and pans clanging
like she's producing a song.
R&B blasts through the speakers, a long instrumental plays.

Enough time for Mama to clear her throat,
enough time to make my way to our galley kitchen.

I lean along the entryway as she salts the water in a large pot,
grabs a black slotted spoon when the lyrics start,
and lifts it to her mouth, sings.

Her singing voice is raspy, more Erykah than Jill,
she keeps the spoon to her lips as a mic,
moving about the kitchen until she notices me.

How long have you been there?
she shouts over the music, smiling.

> *Just this verse.*

She nods, picks up a seasoned, thinly sliced
chicken breast and adds it to a cast iron,
jumps back into the song at the chorus.

I join her in singing, in seasoning,
both of us with little space
to move around.

But we make do.

The water boils.
I pass her the box of cavatappi,
she passes me the salt to return to the cabinet.

I grab the plates,
she stirs the noodles
and flips the chicken for a perfect sear.

> *What's got you in a good mood?* I ask.

Sometimes you just gotta make it good.

I hear the stress in her voice
but she jumps right into our favorite song to skate to,
"Square Biz" by Teena Marie. This one more upbeat, joyful.

Jaelyn, go get our skates,
she calls out as I'm setting
the dinner table for two.

> *To do what with?*
> I know she doesn't think we're skating right now.

To skate! Girl, get my skates.

I don't question her again
and grab our skates out of the hall closet.

I deliver her pair first.
Black with red laces
and red wheels that flash each time they roll.

She bubbles with excitement
and lowers the heat on the heavy cream,
then slips her bare feet into her skates.

I turn my face up at her lack of socks,
go grab myself a pair,
hurry back to the hall closet and put mine on.

This is foolish.

My mama is already twisting and turning,
moving her feet swiftly but carefully
to the tempo, making sure not to interfere with our dinner.

Come on!
she says as she sways and snaps.

So don't you have no doubt,
I'm gonna spell it out,
Teena Marie sings.

I skate into the kitchen and join her
on the tile, fall in line
with a routine she just made up.

Kick kick spin,
slide to the left,
step right over left,

left over right
right over left,
left over right.

It's simple
but enough
to get lost in.

After a few repetitions,
my mama stops skating,
pours some pasta water
into the cream to thicken it.
Then she shakes more spices in.

Her cooking is hard to follow.
Like a lot of Black families,
she doesn't go by strict measurements,
just goes by judgment. Heart.

It's all to taste,
she would say.

My mama hits every song note as she stirs the cream,
water, and seasoning together.

She notices my leaning against the counter,
how I've already grown tired of our performance.

What's wrong?

> *I just am not in the mood to hear
> music that reminds me of the rink.*

She sighs, turns it down a bit.

*It reminds me of the rink, too.
But it's out of our control. You can either
let everything steal your joy
or realize the only thing in your control is your joy.*

I nod and take it in.

Even when our washer is down,

even when the rink is closing,

even when we're forced to downgrade our living space,

my mama always keeps a smile.

She increases the volume,

mixes the noodles and sauce together,

allows a quick simmer,

and seasons to taste.

Five

TWENTY-TWO DAYS UNTIL WESTSIDE ROLL CLOSES

As I exit the movie theater,
a car's bass bumps,
the frame rattles from vibrations.

Everyone who works here is used to this:
people using our lot
to do anything but park for a movie.

The sun is aggressive against my face,
but I can still see Noelle is driving the bass-bumping car.
It's definitely not hers.

Noe? I shout as I walk toward it.

She leans over,
rolls the passenger window down.

Get in, we going to a cookout!

Whose car is this?

    I ask as I open
    the creaky door,
    inspecting every spot,
    clocking the Black Ice Little Trees air freshener.

Deon's, duh. The only guy
I talk to with a car.

    Who is Deon?

Deon, *Deon. Can you get in?*

I still don't know who Deon is, but I hop in.
Noe changes guys like she changes hairstyles.
Today, her black-and-blond feed-in braids reach her mid back.

    Why didn't you tell me you were coming?

I didn't want you to back out.

    I wasn't gonna back out, I say,
    rolling the window down
    even though she's right.

Seems like Deon doesn't have AC.

You sure weren't, because it's in
our neighborhood. And I brought
you something to wear.

Noe plays our joint playlist,
"Pretty Girl Summer."

We add songs whenever
there's a new cute one
by our favorite woman rappers.

The wind whips in and out
like skaters in a crowd.

My eyes water from the pressure,
Noe's shirt billows like a flag.

We rap the lyrics
like we penned the songs
ourselves.

Right now, it feels like old times.
The motions of us together as familiar
as the line dances
Black folks are practically born knowing.

Right now, there aren't any worries.

We pull up to a subdivision

that's a short drive from our apartment complex.

The one-story ranch houses are so close together
only a sliver of yard rests between them.

Almost every parking spot is taken—
cars in the grass, some against the curb.

Noe lowers the music, finds a spot,
and we pull the sun visors down to check our looks.

Papers fall from mine—old mail, a registration.

> *Whoever Deon is needs to clean up,*
> I say.

Because this is a messss,
Noe finishes.

She applies her Fenty gloss,
pops her lips,
applies again,
then hands the gloss to me.

We've always shared everything:
lip gloss, clothes, money when the other
doesn't have it, my mama and her grandma.

The backyard is full of kids shouting,
running through the water hose.

Girls sit in lawn chairs.
Some men take point at the grill.
The boys our age take point at the snack table.

There goes some of the team,
Noe says, and points toward her friends.

They're dressed like they're going to a school dance.

Gold jewelry on their wrists and necks,
bundles wand-curled and slightly windblown,
cute minidresses and lace-up sandals.

I look down at myself:
a crop top that doesn't reveal anything,
though I don't have much to show,
a skirt that's a little loose because I don't have curves,
Old Navy sandals from last summer.

> *Why didn't you say they were coming?* I ask.
> *I would have invited friends, too.*

Friends is a stretch.
I mean Trey or the people I join skate lines with
who barely know my name.

It'll be cool, I promise.

I follow Noe as she hands out hugs
like Halloween candy, not missing a single person.
She introduces me to Deon,
his brothers, his uncles, his cousins.

Deon finally points us to the food
and we stack our plates high
with chicken and brats and hot dogs
macaroni and baked beans.

We take our seats
next to Kaila, Ashley,
Asha, and some others.

They laugh
and eat
and laugh.

I try to join the conversation
but they're telling stories about Noe
that I'm hearing for the first time.

I get names mixed up.

> *Are they talking about Deon or Rashad?*
> I lean over and ask Noe.

Deon. Girl, you gotta keep up.
We talk fast, she says.

I sit back in my seat,
eat quietly.

The sun has just about set
and the backyard lights activate.
Deon stands in the middle.

Aye, y'all.
We about to bring three tables out
for Spades. Who wants smoke?

The dance team, including Noe,
raise their hands.

I've never learned Spades.
My mama's not a card player,
and my dad never felt like teaching me.

Deon's uncles drag the card tables
into the middle of the grass.

Had I known all of y'all were coming,
we would have had the cookout at Riverside Park,
one of Deon's uncles says to no one in particular,
a Black & Mild tucked in his mouth.

Noe and her friends, and four other teams of two
dart toward the tables, claim their seats,
stare their partners and opponents down.

Instead of rooting Noe on,
I move farther away.

I find a seat where I can hide in the shadows,
forgotten like the discarded cups and plates littering the yard.

The wireless speaker that was once low
is now blaring cookout classics.

Deon's auntie gets up from her lawn chair,
dances next to it.

Oooo, what y'all know about this?
I want to join her.
It reminds me of my mama.
It reminds me of Thursday Soul Nights
but I'm bound to my seat.

My eyes fall on Noe
as she slams a card down.
She and Kaila high-five across the table.

Then the ultimate cookout song starts,
the three defining notes of "Before I Let Go"
by Frankie Beverly and Maze
gets all of us on our feet.

I surprise myself when I congregate
with everyone else in the middle
of the yard near the Spades tables
and join the Electric Slide.

We beam at each other,
make new facial expressions with each turn,
like we're auditioning for a part.

Once we're facing the back of the house,
I recognize the girl beside me.
It's Tiana from the rink.

The song ends and we fall out of line.

Sweaty. Breathless. Joy on our mouths.

Hey, Tiana.

I wince the moment
the hushed *hey* leaves my lips.

My body stiffens
like clothing that hang-dried too long.
I doubt she remembers my name.

Hey. Jaelyn, right?
she asks.

Yeah.

Who'd you come here with?

I point to Noe, who has resorted
to yelling at the other team.

Tiana's eyebrows rise at Noe's big motions
and even bigger voice. We share a laugh
and she throws her knotless braids into a ponytail.

You? I ask.

*I know one of Deon's cousins,
we kinda grew up together.*
She points to him.

Can you believe the rink is closing?
Tiana asks.

No. I feel like I'm losing a part of me.

Well, we are.

We slip into conversation
like we've ever said more
than a handful of words to each other.

We devour a second plate
then a third,
reminding each other
of good times at WestSide Roll.

We talk so long
the half-moon climbs the sky.

Six

SEVENTEEN DAYS UNTIL WESTSIDE ROLL CLOSES

Trey: Can we skip the rink tomorrow?

Me: You that scared to skate?

Trey: Nahhh you tryna be funny

Me: Why are we skipping?

Trey: It's a surprise

Me: So you like surprises? Noted

Trey: I mean we don't have to

Trey again: There was just this dope place
I wanted to take you. Tomorrow maybe. I think you'd like it.

Trey again: I put all my friends on
but I forgot, you don't explore
outside the West Side

Me: That's not true

Trey: Prove it then

Me: Well you know I'm not missing
any more nights at the rink. Come get me now.

I stand in front of the mirror,
smooth my palms over the pink two-piece skirt set
that my mama might not let me wear.

> *Mama, can you come here?*
> I yell from my room.

She can't stand it when I do that,
but my feet are planted
in the carpet.

Me and Trey have only hung out
on accident or a couple hours at a time.
Nervousness creeps
into my system.

The more we hang,
the more I want to see him.

Jaelyn, you look beautiful,
my mama says when she walks in,
pink bonnet and matching robe on.

I'll take these off when he comes in,
she says, standing behind me.

> *When he comes in?*

*You thought I was going to let some
nugget head drive off with my baby?*

My mama meeting Trey makes me even more anxious.

She grabs the necklace my dad gave me
years ago from my dresser,
gold with a daisy charm,
lays it on my chest before clasping it.

I stopped wearing it when they divorced,
but she's always loved it on me.
I place my hand over it, get used to the jewelry again.

The first date is weird, but it's easy.
If you like each other, the conversation will flow.

    And if we don't?

Well, you can give it another try
or you can leave it be.

He knocks on the door / like he needs the whole neighborhood / to hear him / maybe he likes / an audience / maybe that eases his nerves / but I need / deep breaths and affirmations / I tell myself / this will be good / it'll be like the other times / we've hung out.

Are you going to get that? / my mama asks / then notices / I can't budge / she hurries to answer it / and I finally move / to the bedroom door / My mama snatches off her robe / bonnet / slides her long-sleeved T-shirt / over her reddish-brown skin / to cover the arm / she donated plasma from / today / $80 for the first donation / $50 for the second / and $20 each session after / She hasn't donated / since the divorce was finalized / when we were desperate / she opens the door / says *Come on in* / he strolls inside / with the biggest smile.

I creep into the living room

as he thanks my mama for letting

him take me out. He glances at the yellow

place mats on the dining table. His eyes catch

the painting of four Black women

getting pedicures from four Black men,

the one my dad hated,

now hanging by the portraits

of me in each grade.

He laughs, asks me,

This is what's expected, huh?

My mama barely lets him sit down before she starts:

How old are you?
How old are you really?
I'm making sure you ain't lying.
Do you plan to go to college?
Do your parents know you're here?
Do they know you're taking my daughter out?
How long have y'all known each other?
Did she tell you she has a curfew?
  11 p.m., not a second later.
If she's not home on time, I'm going to find you.
If I search your name on Indiana Case Search, what will I find?

  The last question brings quiet.
  Trey fidgets with his keys, runs his finger
    over the silver ridges.

I'm joking, Mrs. Coleman,
he says, chuckling a little.

Any other time, she'd have her arms folded,
a scowl on her face.
But his charm works on her, too.

Well, y'all have a good time.
I don't want to hold you up.

We walk to his car

and I don't open my mouth
for fear I'll talk too fast.

I keep smoothing my outfit,
and Trey, in his linen shirt
and striped shorts, does the same.

He opens the passenger door.
Your hooptie awaits.

He waits until I'm in
then lightly jogs to the driver's side.

Trey talks the whole ride,
barely takes a breath, voice shaky,
his words an avalanche tumbling out.
I finally stop him.

> *Trey.* I place my hand on his right.
> *You can calm down. It's just me.*

It's weird being the person calming someone else down.

You right, he says. His shoulders relax,
he slumps into the driver's seat.
But you're more than "just me."

We pull into Fountain Square,
close-ish to downtown Indy,
only a few people walking the strip of shops and restaurants.

Fountain Square is a hipster area with a vintage feel.
In other words, Black people my age
don't hang out here much.

Most of the stores aren't owned by us,
most of the shoppers don't look like us.

Black people hang out downtown,
sometimes at the mall or the canal walk,
where the buildings aren't red brick
but reinforced concrete and Indiana limestone.

Trey swivels the car into a tight spot.

Look how I whipped the car.

    You didn't do anything.

You are such a hater, he says, laughing.

When we get out,
he points to the strip of shops
directly across the street,
yellow paint outlining
its glass windows and doors.

Bee Vinyl is over there.

After you, madam,
he says as he opens the shop door.
He couldn't be more silly if he tried.

I sing along to the song playing,
bobbing my head to the beat.

Look at you, already liking the store.

> *Don't start*, I say.

*I know there used to be a vinyl store
in your neighborhood, so I brought you here.*

> *To gentrified neighborhood number two?*
> I ask.

Well. He brushes his hand over his curls.
Bee Vinyl is Black-owned, at least.

The few customers in here—
a white girl in all leather,
an older Black woman in a floral blouse,
a teen boy with shaggy hair—
are engrossed in the bins.

The checkered floor holds our feet,
small plants grace shelves,
the sweet aroma of coffee swarms,
colorful string lights line a small stage.

The seventies vibe—from the records on the wall
to the boho light fixtures
to the thrifted retro chairs—is breathtaking.

My dad took me to record stores all the time,
searching for rare CDs or something new
to blast in the living room on any given day,

so we could dance   dance   dance
mumble the words until we learned every lyric,
got every note.

I haven't been to one since.

We stop in front of the neo-soul records,
me flipping through one stack, him flipping through another,
my index finger stroking the plastic as I admire classics.

I noticed you love music.
So I thought I'd put you on.

He doesn't look up at me, keeps hunting.

And I collect vinyls.

    Collect?
    I ask.

Yeah, collect and listen to.
I'm not one of those fake
music lovers, buying them
just to say I have them.

What's wrong with that?
I'm offended for the non-listeners.

It's not authentic.
If I love an artist,
I'm going to listen to them.

    That's what streaming is for.
    There's nothing wrong with having vinyls just because.

His eyebrows rise so high
they almost leave his face,
mouth in an O shape.

Wow, I thought you were a music fan for real.
He waves his hand.

    I suck my teeth. *Oh, whatever.*

We move down the row,
now in the R&B section.
Trey pulls Ari Lennox's *age/sex/location* vinyl
from its snug place.

Now, this my wife.

    Boy, she's not thinking about you.

Yeah, yeah, yeah.

He takes the record to the register
and leans over the counter, whispering to the cashier.

They laugh like old friends.

"Boy Bye" by Ari Lennox and Lucky Daye
starts, and Trey's smile is as long as the downtown canal.

He dances toward me.
What you know about this?

> *What do you know?*
> I ask back.

He has no clue that I've listened
to every cover of every song on this album,
pictured myself having the exact exchange
of the duo in the song:

Ari and Lucky pretend to be strangers
who meet during a night out and instantly connect.
They laugh and joke with each other.
Ari denies her desire. Lucky Daye knows she likes him.

Trey gets closer to me, stomps his foot rhythmically,
extends one arm out and swings it to his right,
extends the other and swings it to his left,
like he's in a nineties R&B group.

> *This ain't even that type of song,* I say.

Girl, this is soul.

He keeps on with his routine
like he's not in the middle of a record store
making a fool of himself
for the three others and employees to see.

Dance with me? he asks.

>*Looking like that?* I scoff. *Absolutely not.*

Aw, come on. No one's judging you.
Hit a little two-step with me.

I'm not just worried about people judging.

I'm worried about getting too close,
of more expectations,
the ability to hurt or be hurt,
leave or be left.

Distance is easy.
I can't catch feelings from afar.

Before I can object again
he pulls me in,
begins to two-step
so I can ease into the rhythm.

Come on, you know you love this song.

I loosen up, tell myself, *It's just two-stepping.*
I fall in line as if we're skating.
I've watched my parents two-step,
admired how they understood each other's feet.

Trey stares into my eyes
like he's uncovering the mystery of me.
I tear my eyes away, find the vinyls instead,
feet still moving with his.

Trey's smile becomes mine.
We're body to body now,
his spice and oak intertwining
with my rose and vanilla scent.

Stepping, stepping, stepping to each other's beat.
Trey goes for a dip, both arms cradling me,
his eyes not leaving mine.

I look up at him, can't escape this time.
A thoughtful look replaces his smiling one.
I break the stillness, ask what's keeping him quiet.

He slowly pulls me back up and the song fades out.

We sing the last line together.
And I love all your angles, angles.

Trey never answers.

Trey opens the door for me as we leave,
and I flow through quietly,
into the muggy outdoor air.

> *You made me get out of bed to put on a show?*

Did you have fun?
he quips.

I pause, trying to figure out
how to tell him yes without
making his head big.

> *Want to walk a little before we go?*

I want to keep the chocolate-sweet
energy whirring between us.

He opens his mouth to speak

but no words come out,

then he grins

big and goofy.

He musters up, *Yeah.*

We start walking,
Fountain Square still calm.
Our steps slow,
steady,
matching.

Why do you like this area so much?

*Me and the only other Black people from school
used to come here because everyone
else didn't really mess with us,* he says.
*They'd go to a coffee shop by the school,
but we'd drive here when we really wanted to get away.*

Do you still have friends from there?

Something like that.
He rubs his palms against his shorts.

What kind of answer is that?
It slips out before I think.

We turn down a fork in the road,
roaming past glass windows
with painted bubble letters.

Not you calling me out.

Not you being cagey.

He's thinking, chews his lip and brushes his hand down his neck.

*If you call friends people you check on sometimes
but don't maintain a real relationship with, then I guess.
But I don't feel like friends should abandon you.*

Abandon you how?

He sighs.
He seems frustrated,
not with me, but with something
out of his control.

I mean, it's almost like I don't exist to them.

    I'm sorry. So I guess you don't miss them? I ask.

I miss what I thought our friendship would be after I left.

    That makes a lot of sense.
    I say, peering into a bookstore.

What do you miss?
he asks, face on the glass next to me.

    Oh, so we're going for the hard-hitting questions?
    Our breath leaves a cloud on the window.

You just asked me the deepest ones yet, he says.

    Deepest? Those barely scratch the surface.

I would hate to see what you actually *want to ask.*

                       Me too, I think.

Are you going to answer my question?

    I plead the Fifth, I say, and laugh.

He laughs with me, nudges me with his elbow.
Trey's so much taller than me that when I nudge back,
my elbow is only in his lower arm.

I do have a question, though, he says.

> *Wassup?*

He hesitates, leaves the glass
to start walking again. I fall in step beside him.

Was just gonna make sure you had fun.

I can tell the real question
burns inside of him.

> *I did, I would do it again.*

We face each other on my porch.

It's dark, but folks are still out
bike riding, talking.

This neighborhood is always lively,
moves to its own noise.

I don't want this night to end,
he says.

> *I can ask my mama*
> *if we can sit on the porch,*
> I say, knowing she might say no.

Would you really?
He places his hand on his cheek,
looks up at the sky like he's watching Cupid fly above us.
Awwww.

I roll my eyes and run inside,
heart pounding
with want.

I knock on my mama's shut door.

What's going on, Jaelyn?

> *Do you mind if I sit on the porch for a little bit?*

Silence. I imagine she's checking the time.

You got thirty minutes.

    Thanks,
    I shout over my shoulder,
    already halfway to the door.

I bring out two lawn chairs,
place them side by side, sit in one,
and invite him to the other.

We look up at the stars,
heads craned, feet kicked out.

We stare into the sky
like it's a map to decipher,
silent for minutes and minutes.

The crackling of cicadas
moving in the trees
keeps time.

His hand inches
toward my lawn chair,
grazes my fingers.

Seven

THIRTEEN DAYS UNTIL WESTSIDE ROLL CLOSES

Monthly Sunday dinner at Granny's
means the minute me and my mama
walk in, we're bombarded

by enough seasonings to make us sneeze
and the supersweet smell of vanilla
because she'll always bake a cake, too.

Food's almost ready,
Mrs. Joyce shouts from the kitchen
as we settle at the dining table.

You need help with anything, Mama?
my mama asks, knowing Mrs. Joyce
can't stand someone else in her kitchen.

Granny never corrects her
calling her mama like she's her own,
says she's ours as long as we'll have her.

I'm good, Granny responds. But I peek into the kitchen,
notice her trembling, slow movements,
wonder if I'm imagining things.

Noe grabs the plates.
I grab the fancy burgundy place mats
we only use for our dinners.

We set the table for four
without speaking.

The spread is a miracle.
Catfish fried crispy,
collard greens in a bed of spicy juice,
baked macaroni with a perfectly crusted top.

We pass the dishes like collection plates
at Sunday service after receiving the word,
overdo it on our helpings.

How was the cookout the other day?
Mrs. Joyce asks.

The food was fire,
Noe says.

> *But not as good as yours,*
> I chime in.

Hmmph, Noe grunts across from me,
then eats a forkful
of catfish, macaroni, and greens.

I take a bite, too.
We haven't spoken
since I left Noe with her friends
at the cookout and rode home with Tiana.

I didn't see a problem,
I let her know we were leaving
while she held down the Spades table.

Hmmph what? I ask
once I'm done chewing.

My mama and Mrs. Joyce
look between us.

Just didn't seem like you had fun.

I sigh.

How so? Did you check on me?

All right, enough.
What's going on?
my mama asks.

Mrs. Joyce sucks hot sauce from her fingers.
Why are y'all arguing over a cookout?

Nobody's arguing, we say in unison.

Okay, so cut it, my mama says.
Y'all are sisters.

I blink hard to keep
from rolling my eyes.
Noe rolls hers,
gets out her phone

which isn't allowed at our dinners,
scrolls like she's searching for an answer.
Sunday dinners used to be our favorite part of the month.

It's where we hear the best stories
about who Mrs. Joyce was
before now, who my mama was
before my dad.

Afterward, me and Noe would coop up in her room,
exchange *Girl, I can't believe my mama used to . . .*
or *Girl, I can't believe my granny used to . . .*

Now
I'll probably go home with my mama,
then go days without talking to Noe.

*Anyway. The changes around
here are happening so quickly.*
My mama says with a half-empty plate beneath her.
Only the greens have survived so far.

Have you tried any of the new businesses yet?

I got myself some flowers the other day, my mama says.
*The two women in there didn't greet me when I walked in,
just watched me.*

A shame that they come to our neighborhood acting like that,
Mrs. Joyce says.

I pull my phone out,
text Trey,
Tiana,

tune out the rest
of the conversation.

The only text I have is from my dad,
who I never responded to.

Hey baby girl. Are you free Saturday?
I'd love to see you . . .

Have you heard this song?

He sends a link to an artist I've heard of
but never listened to.

I slide my phone back in my pocket,
taking my turn to play ghost,

and shift my weight
toward my mama

so I don't have to look
in Noe's direction.

Hours later, it's time for Sunday Skate.

My mama and I pull up to the rink and the lot is already packed.
Usually Sunday is for oldheads, but Mr. Mike opened it to all ages.

The cars glisten for attention, yellows and royal purples,
rims spinning, sound systems bumping underneath cars, glowing
   lights on each side.

The cops I've started to spot more haven't arrived yet. They only
   used to surveil Saturday Skate
because "eighteen and under" sometimes means fights and
   parking lot beef.

Now they're here every skate night. They assume the darker it is,
   the worse we are.

Me and my mama walk through the rink
like Noe and I usually do, skates in hand,
ready to unleash the problems
we've tamed all week.

Long time no see, Baby Roller,
someone shouts from the arcade.
My mama turns, curly hair flipping
with the snap of her neck.

What? Ronny Glide? Look at you.

She prances to him,
one arm outstretched for a side hug,
the other cradling her skates.
And on it goes.

After she speaks to almost everyone here,
we head toward the lockers.

We don't waste time getting on the rink floor
'cause every minute counts.

We skate side by side, doing stunts,
sometimes mirroring each other.

Our tricks are like us,
so similar with a few small differences.

Hers are bigger, boisterous, yearning to be seen,
and there's a softness to her moves I haven't quite grasped.

We flow with each other like a current.

But my joy fades quickly.
The back of a familiar body
is right
in front of me.

I haven't seen him in a year.

He glides through the rink, sweat towel in his back pocket.

I turn and my mama is no longer at my side.
I look between bodies
on the congested rink floor.

And now I've lost sight of him, too.

>   My anger
>   threatens to overflow.
>   My feet move
>   but I'm
>   floating

        floating

>   gone.

You been hiding from me?

Trey comes out of nowhere,
throws his arm around my shoulder.

Sunday nights are too packed to teach,
but Trey said he'd meet me here anyway.

I don't answer him,
my eyes darting around for my father.

Trey grabs my hand
and leads me to the arcade,
away from the loudness.

A cop stands to the side of the arcade,
hands on his holster,
waiting.
Watching.

There are five in total,
way more than the two security guards
who hold it down any other day.

This is what the downtown mall
looked like when they started enforcing rules
to keep us from going:

No groups larger than three.
No teens after 6 p.m. unless with a parent or guardian.
No loitering.

We sit in identical game chairs,

his hands on the steering wheel like he's ready
to drive us out of here. And I'd let him.

I smooth my hair into its puff
to make sure the edge control is doing its job.

You look good tonight, he says, attention
on me instead of the trial screen.

    Thank you. I tried.

I was thinking, I'd like to take you to the movies.

    Ugh, I do not want to be reminded of my job.

I mean the drive-in. Big screen,
some privacy, lots of snacks.
My nice-looking face.

I contemplate,
steer the trial-screen car.

    I like the sound of that.

Just me and Trey, and Betsy.

I'm nervous to be alone again,
what that will mean
for the feelings taking root.

A disco song I've never heard plays.

And now louder than the song are skaters shouting and clapping, voices and hands in unison like a choir.

We walk over to see the cause of the commotion, and it's my parents

> battling in the middle of the floor
> as if they haven't fought enough.

They're fire. Wait, is that your mom?
Trey asks.

I sink into myself,
body curved like a shrimp,
and bury my face in my hands.

> Yes, and my dad,
> I say, wincing.

Oh, so that's *how you learned to skate.*

My mama and dad   bend
                  to each other's bodies,
in sync like a seasoned girl group.

The neon lights put on their own show,
flashes synced to each beat.
The overhead lights are dimmed.

Seeing them battle
stirs up memories
sweet and bitter.

My birthday parties here: ten kids, two pizzas, and thirty arcade
    tokens each.
Their last fight before the divorce was final.
Me and my dad dancing in the living room, my mama joining in.
The last day I saw him, when I didn't know it'd be the last.

Seeing him

        drowning in sweat

feet shuffling

        joy radiating from his body

makes me want to hurl
the simmering angry words I've held back
at   his   face

The song ends. The crowd disperses,
overhead lights brightening again.
Each mark on the shiny rink floor
shows itself.

The cops lined against the back
wall watch us like fish in a tank.

I wish them pigs would move,
someone complains behind me.

They're tamping down our free.
We're on edge, the mere sight of them
enough to change our behavior,

keep us from feeling like we can do
or be whatever
on the rink floor.

Trey leads me to the purple barrier wall.
He leans and I lean beside him.

He's gotten better at balance.

You good? he asks.

For a short moment,
my parents weren't at the front
of my mind.

> *Yeah,* I say.

Next thing I know, people are yelling / We turn / see two girls / fighting / swinging on each other / like money was stolen / and then police / pepper spray in the air / I panic / everyone becoming / a blur / I snatch / the collar of my shirt / over my nose and mouth / the two girls get snatched / from the crowd / by their arms / cops dragging them / and anyone else / who dares / Trey grabs me / by my hand / pulls / I try to stop him / unlace my skates / but he shouts / *Come on* / I wonder / about my mama / and dad / how I'll find them / I wonder / how this night went from bad / to even worse / It's pandemonium / my heart racing / legs moving faster / than I can keep up with / Fights are everywhere / now / people are trampling / yelling / grabbing / we're finally outside / skating toward the car / hoping the cops don't decide / to arrest us all.

Like mothers always do,
she finds me—Trey's right hand in mine in the parking lot—
and grabs my other to yank us toward her car.

People run in different directions,
rental skates strewn near the entrance
like fallen streamers.

But my car—
Trey starts to debate.

Listen, I know I'm not your mama, but get in this car,
she says with gritted teeth,
the kind of statement you don't question
out of a Black mama's mouth.

He hops in the back seat
and before we buckle in,
she peels off,

passing everyone still outside yelling
at each other for safety.

When we get to our complex,
a few people are crowded in a circle
sharing a blunt, smoke billowing in the air around them
like they've made a campfire.

This is what it's like around here in summer.
Black folks enjoying the weather, dodging a few truths:

Every day, a neighbor rents a U-Haul to leave.
Every day, more cop cars creep down the streets.
Every day means new joggers, funny looks, dog walkers.

Jaelyn! Ruby!
I know that deep voice from anywhere.

Quentin, why are you here?
You don't show up any other time,
my mama says, but continues walking,
my dad's footsteps heavy behind us.

He catches up at our front door.

Just give me five minutes with Jaelyn.
His voice disturbs the cloudless sky.

After all this time, all you want
is five minutes with your daughter?
Jaelyn, how do you feel?
'Cause, Q, you're not gonna come over here
upsetting my baby.

This is my worst nightmare.
Trey barely knows me,
doesn't know anything
about the divorce.

I feel like your timing could not be worse, I say.
My voice lands harsh, gritty.

Jaelyn, I've been trying
to talk to you for weeks.
You haven't answered me.

Because I don't have anything good to say,
I mumble, my jaw clenching.

The tension is thick as grits.

My dad throws his arms up.
All right, I'm trying, Jaelyn.

Not hard enough,
my mama says.

I'm going inside now,
I say.

I don't look at him,
just walk to the porch,
push my key into the lock,
and step inside
with my mama and Trey
right behind me.

Part of me regrets not saying more.

I could have told him all the ways I've needed him

in the past couple of years.

I needed to share music with him.

I needed his help finding a job.

I needed his pep talk when math got too hard.

I needed him at the first sign of me and Noelle falling apart.

I need him, right now, to tell me if Trey's feelings are real.

If I should keep going.

I could have told him all of the ways

I've shied away from people because of him,

avoided getting close.

But he should already know he hurt me,

that I deserve much better than this.

Once we're inside,
I take a pool-deep breath in, let it rush out.

My mama looks at Trey and says,
I'll take you back to your car
when everything cools down.

She goes to her room
and slams her door.

I want to do the same,
but Trey's puppy dog eyes
grab my attention.

Are you okay?

> *I don't even know.*
> I shake my head.

He grabs me up in a hug,
squeezes tight like I'm a stress ball,
trying to force my disappointment out.

My head finds comfort on his chest.
I melt into him as he rocks me.

Dads are the worst sometimes,
he says.

> *Yeah, they are.*

Eight

TEN DAYS UNTIL WESTSIDE ROLL CLOSES

Trey's tires rumble against the gravel
at the Tibbs Drive-In. We haven't moved
our joined damp hands from the center console,
warmth flowing between us.

And we haven't seen each other since Sunday Skate.

I've been embarrassed.

He's texted me
asking how I've slept,
if I want to talk about anything.

I give him short answers:

Fine I guess
thanks for checking but no

But tonight,
I'm going to forget it all.

It's my and Trey's second date.

The sun sets behind large screens,
hues of blue and pink spread across
the sky like watercolors, car lights reminiscent of a big city.

He pulls into a parking spot,
changes to the correct radio station,
and turns to me.

Concession time?

We're unusually quiet as we walk over.

My mind races to break the ice.

    So I take it you enjoyed our last date? I ask.

So I take it you did, too? he asks back.

    I asked first.

I stop in the gravel,
admire how the sunset paints
his brown skin, makes it warm.

I asked you out again because you're the coolest girl I know.

He shoves his hands in his pockets,
steps side to side while he speaks.

*And beautiful. You're fun. You can skate
your ass off. You care so much
about everything. And your smile
lights up a room, man.*

His voice trails off as if he's writing
a poem about me.

Each time we're together
my body threatens to unspool
all of me at his feet.

~ 142 ~

Trey keeps the nachos between us.
He convinced me to try loaded 'cause "they're heat,"
but I'm a nacho-and-cheese-only type.

Tell me these ain't good, he says
in the middle of a romantic scene.

> *Shh*, I say as Issa Rae
> stands in her awkwardness,
> much like me,
> and tells the guy she's falling.

Trey fills a nacho with everything
and lifts it to my mouth.
I open, eyes glued to the screen,
thinking about how opposite we are.

How I can watch a movie in silence
and he has a comment every two seconds.

How he likes loaded nachos
and I prefer plain.

> *I could hang with you all day*,
> I say, twisting in my seat
> to stare at him.

For once, I've forgotten
about the rink, my family, Noelle.

Spending time with Trey has been the fun
I needed, has saved me
from the things I can't control.

How about a lot of days? he asks,
feeds me another nacho like he didn't
just say what I want
but won't let myself have.

In the middle of the movie,

he says, *We should play twenty-one questions.*

> *You have twenty-one questions for me?*

More, he says,
smile snow white.

I've never seen him frown,
even when he can't get his footing while we skate.

> *Okay, you start. And please know
> that we'll need to see this movie again.*

He laughs.
*We already know the ending, though.
They have to end up together.*

> *You know what? I'll start.
> Why do you talk during movies?*

Because it's the best time to share my commentary!

I shake my head.

Why don't you?
he asks.

> *Because I like to enjoy each scene.*

Do you love love?
His whole body faces me,

seat pushed back
for his long legs.

> *What a jump. I thought twenty-one questions*
> *was supposed to start off simple.*

I fidget with my nails,
rip at them like orange peels.

You can be as simple as you want.
I'd like the nitty-gritty.

> *That's a hard question.*
> I lean my seat back to meet his.

What's hard about it?

> *I mean, I love the thought of love.*
> *But I've never been in love.*

> *Have you?*
> I ask back.

I've been in like.
I had a girlfriend.
He scrapes cheese up with a broken
tortilla chip, careful not to break it even more.

> *So, what made you in like*
> *but not in love?*

Now who's asking the deep questions?

You started this! I say.

Love is something you can't explain. Trey stops to chew.
*One day someone comes out of nowhere
and completely turns your world around,
makes you look at every day or everything differently.*

And like?
I grab a tortilla chip.
It breaks instantly.

*Twenty-one questions is supposed
to be back and forth.*
He laughs.

Okay, next two are yours, then.

He shrugs.
*Fair.
Like is when they make you happy,
you're excited to see them,
but if you lost them,
you wouldn't be crushed.*

I give him a second,
make sure he doesn't have any dying
commentary to add.

> *I think when you love someone,* I say, *you try your hardest not to hurt them. You make every moment count.*
> *You show up.*

He nods,
gazes out the window
at the big screen.

Sounds like both of us
have experienced a person
who didn't show up.

> *Who, your last girlfriend?*

Yeah.

> *Would you do it again?*

Me and her?

> *No, a girlfriend in general.*

If the other person in the car wanted that.

I look out my window at all the cars, Jeeps and Chevy Impalas and Nissan Altimas experiencing the same movie we are, lined up in the parking lot like dominoes.

> *Which car?*

Jae, stop playing,
he says, and laughs

but won't look at me.
What do you want?
We've been hanging out a lot.

I wish we hadn't finished all the snacks.
I need something to delay the conversation.

> *Do you want to know today?*
> I ask to buy more time.

Are you trying to find a way to reject me nicely?
I've experienced worse if that's the case. It would be no hard fee—

> *I like you, Trey.*

Oh.

> *A lot more than I expected to*
> *or wanted to, really.*

Why didn't you want to like me?
I find that hard to believe.
He smirks.

Everything is a joke to him,
but I appreciate the levity.

> *I've seen what failed love looks like.*
> *I don't think I want to take part in it.*

You think I'll fail you?

> I huff.
>
> *I think I can fail you.*

Who says someone has to hurt?
he asks.

> *Everyone. I've never seen differently.*
> *Look at the movie,*
> I say, point to the screen.
> *Even Issa's crying.*

Trey looks out the windshield
at the heartbreak scene,
his mouth twisted to the left.

His cheek rests on his palm.

I get it,
he says.
I can't be mad at that.

The movie goes on,
our questions don't.

When we get to my apartment door,

mosquitoes buzz around
my porch light, lightning bugs
goldening the trees nearby.

The light casts a shadow on
my face, makes Trey's bright.

Even when the rink is gone,
we have to keep this going,
he says.
'Cause I don't plan on failing you.

With his words I'm a candle,
burning down to my most vulnerable parts.
I let go of his hands and check my phone for the time.

    I have two minutes.

That's long enough:
Can I kiss you?

My breath catches.
I nod yes,
and he presses his hand
to the back of my neck,

brings my face close, and kisses me,
his plump lips fitting perfectly between mine.

It feels like everything I've imagined a kiss to be.

It's soft, causing a wave of heat in my limbs.
It feels like I am whirling.
It feels like I have levitated.

I rush into my room
and FaceTime Noelle.

Sometimes, it feels like we're reaching
for each other but can never connect,
fingertips begging to touch.

But she's the only person
I have when it comes to boy advice.

Please pick up,
I whisper to myself.

She does, sitting in the dark,
TV blasting, its blue light
flashing on her face.

Wassup? she asks,
then turns *The Real Housewives of Potomac* down.

Her voice is low, weary,
a shakiness to it that I haven't heard
since her last big breakup a year ago.

    Are you good? I ask.

Yeah, wassup?
Noe says.

    You sure?

Jae, yes.

I don't really wanna talk about it.

    Okay . . . well. When you're ready.

What's going on?

    I wanted to talk about Trey.

    With my first crush,
    a guy on the basketball team
    who didn't know I existed,
    Noe entertained my delusions,
    guided my daily outfits,
    gave me a script for every possible scenario.
    But with Trey, someone I spend most of my time with,
    she doesn't ask
    So what happened today? like she used to.
    She doesn't say
    This about to be your man! like she used to.

Go ahead.

    I think I want to be his girlfriend.
    But I'm scared.

Of what? Has he hurt you?
She turns to the camera for a moment.

    No. But he could.

And I could win a million dollars.
But I haven't.

    Not yet . . .

Jae, why can't you follow your heart?
Take a page out of my book.

    But your breakups
    are so heavy.

And? Then they get lighter,
she quips.

    What if he—

I let myself fall deep because
I've already lost people
closest to me. Nothing else
can feel worse.

I try to examine her face,
but she's propped her phone
to the side so I can only see her silhouette.

    Why are you talking like that?

I'm just saying.
Take a chance.

    Umm. Okay.

> *Thanks for the pep talk?*
> *How are you?*
> She's being sketchy.

Jae. I am good!
It's nothing.

> *I'll leave it alone.*
> *You still coming to the rink Saturday?*

Plan on it.

> *All right, love you.*

She hesitates,

housewives arguing in the background.

Me, and my posters, wait for a response that might not come.

Love you always.

SIX DAYS BEFORE WESTSIDE ROLL CLOSES

I'm in my bed,
knowing that the good news
about WestSide Roll I'm waiting for
will never happen.

My mama just called me
into the living room to watch the news
about the rink closing soon,
the reporter's head bobbing as she smiles
about the brewery that will replace it.

My posters stare at me
and I know I look pitiful
in my wrinkled, too-big T-shirt
and Christmas shorts.

I haven't turned on my bedside lamp,
the sun forces itself through
the slits of my bedroom window blinds,
casting white against the darkness.

I've bounced from one social media app
to the other, hoping something
will distract me for more than five minutes.
Instead I get stuck on skate videos from Ron's account:

Mr. Mike and Mr. Kareem doing nutcrackers,
shouting when they land, legs pointing either way,
hands planted on the rink floor.

Tiana striding, her long braids catching
their own rhythm.

The WestSide Riders,
a whistle trilling before they lock arms,
secure themselves to one another like padlocks.

No one tells you that losing a place
feels like someone plunged their fingers
into your chest, snatched your heart out
without permission, leaving you hollow
and wanting.

My mama opens my bedroom door,
and I am a well of tears,
enough to swim in.

The salt teases my lips,
stains my cheeks.
I throw a blanket over my head
to shield her from seeing.

Um, someone named Tiana
is at the door?
she asks more than tells.

Shit.
I gave Tiana my address
when she dropped me off
after the cookout.

Didn't think she'd remember.

I reach my arm out of the blanket,
grab my phone, ignore every text
from everybody, and see Tiana's five.

Her last text reads: Well, it's giving
you're dead so I'm coming to check on you.

Are you okay?
my mama asks,
slippered feet shuffling toward me,
worn sole scraping against the carpet.

I'm fine.

You're not.
The weight of her
drops the end of the bed.
I can tell your friend to leave.

Maybe she should.
I don't want Tiana to see this.

When we skate,
I'm uncontainable.

I spread out
like a dancer who has the floor to themselves.

But right now
I'm so small
she wouldn't recognize me.

> *No, it's okay,*
> I say,

and finally
force myself out of bed.

I open the front door,

and Tiana adjusts her expression of shock
to be indifferent.

My curls hang frizzy and jagged,
little lightning bolts instead of springy coils.

My eyes are cotton ball puffy.

Hey, girl. I've been texting you,
she says.

    My bad.

*You good. I just thought
something happened.*

I step outside,
close the door behind me.

    Wanna walk?
    I ask.

She nods,
leads the way.

    How did you remember where I live?
    I ask as we pass Ezekiel and Jr.
    tossing a football back and forth.

Hi, Jaelyn,
they say in unison.

    Hey, y'all.

Tiana throws them a shy wave,
arm barely raising above her hip.

I live over here, too.

    Since when? Why didn't you say anything?

You didn't ask!
We walk in silence for a few minutes,
kicking rocks in our path, dodging litter
on the broken sidewalk.
What's wrong, though?

    It's just WestSide Roll, I say.

*I get it. And I wasn't even there much until recent.
I take care of my siblings while my mama works,
so I didn't start going anywhere till they got older.*

We pass brick after brick building,
kids lighting fireworks that we'll suffer through
until well past July 4.

After a few minutes, me and Tiana walk
into the corner store attached to the gas station.

The corner store is a staple.
Everyone from the neighborhood

runs in and out of here, only giving the cashiers
small talk unless they're a few cents short.

We grab a couple bags of fifty-cent chips,
some Calypsos,
stand in line,

watch adults buy Swisher Sweets
or a case of Seagram's,
watch kids younger than us
slip Laffy Taffys in their pockets
while one of their friends distracts an employee.

> *I can't believe you eat Fritos,*
> I say to Tiana, frowning.

I can't believe you eat Lay's BBQ chips
instead of Grippo's,
she says.

> *I'm on a budget.*
> *They don't have fifty-cent Grippo's.*

We both laugh.

Nine

TWO DAYS UNTIL WESTSIDE ROLL CLOSES

WestSide Roll feels almost gone tonight.
Is almost gone.

The same people are here for Soul Night
    Tiana
        Mook and Lailani
            Miss Charlene
                Mr. Kareem
                    Mr. Mike
                        DJ Sunny
                            Trey and me

And the same amount of cops from last Sunday.
The same smells waft through the rink.
The same songs play.

I want to hug it all tight,
carry it home, make a replica.

Trey and I stand in the middle of the rink floor,
watch Mook and Mr. Kareem maneuver their bodies
as they teach each other how to big wheel and stride.

The mid-tempo song
allows them to slow their motion,
repeat as many times as needed.

5, 6, 7, 8,
Mook shouts,
and they start again.

I'll never stop being mesmerized by a skater's feet,
how some don't use a toe stop for better dancing.

How some remove their skates in the middle of the floor,
feel the bass tremble through their socked toes before they try
   a move.

Even though that's not allowed,
DJ Sunny looks the other way for regulars.

We gather to watch Mook and Mr. Kareem freestyle
because roller skating ain't a salsa

a two-step
a ballroom dance.

It ain't got no rules to break.

It's what you feel
in your toes, legs, arms.

It's wiggling
bouncing
stepping.

It's a clap
or a whistle around the neck
or a split.

It's magic
you have to work for.

Let's join in,
> I say, and grab Trey's hand.

With my lack of balance?
he asks.

> *You're a quick learner.*
> *You're standing here just fine.*

That's because nobody
is flying past me.

> *Boy, please.*

I skate away from him
to join their line, fall into step,
one, two, three, four,
five, spin, seven, and eight.

I keep missing a kick.

Tiana takes notice,
watches me do the full eight count
before she says,

It's not a kick,
it's more of a roll back and forth.

She repeats the move
with me until I get it,
focused on my feet.

Once I have it,
we throw ourselves
back into the routine.

Trey joins to my right,
misses half the counts,
but doesn't stop trying.

Mr. Mike rolls into the middle,
watches us proudly with his hands on his hips,
smile wide as a billboard.

> *You jumping in, Mr. Mike?*
> I ask.

Nah, a little too tired.

Come on,
Tiana sings.

He sucks his teeth.
Don't have me out here all night.
I got business to take care of.

But we know
once Mr. Mike starts rolling
he won't stop.

He joins our line

and once we hit every movement
precise and pretty

we glide for real
escape the middle of the floor
and stride around the rink

As we shuffle in formation,
more skaters join in

I add my own vibe
snap and sway
let the music lay claim to my body

Trey even has a bounce to him
I didn't teach

Even though Mr. Mike
owns WestSide Roll
he doesn't feel the need to lead

We are all side by side
We are one another's shadows

We are the best traffic

We are a parade

That was my last Thursday Soul Night ever.

Trey clutches the steering wheel,
right hand on the gear.

You ready?
he asks.

I peer out the windshield at WestSide Roll,
the sinking feeling in my stomach
a black hole sucking all the fun we just had.

He takes his hand off the gear,
finds my thigh instead.

What can I do to help?

I don't have an answer.

I fidget in my seat,
turn away from him
and look out the window.

*How about we just sit here
for a little while?*

I don't answer, but he cuts the car off,
rolls the window down,
grabs his phone, and navigates to a playlist.

His palm lies face up
on the center console,
waiting for me to hold it.

I clasp my hand around his and squeeze.

> *I hope you don't think I'm being dramatic.*

You? Never,
he jokes.

> *Stop it,*
> I say, a slight smile in my words.

I know what it feels like to lose a place.
Not exactly in this way,
but I know you're hurting.

I gaze at the painted brick building,
the skaters lingering,
perched between cars
or sprawled out on their hoods.

My phone rings,
and Beth's name scrolls
across the top.

> *Ugh, it's my boss,*
> I mumble.

You gonna answer?
Trey asks.

We both watch it ring together.
My thumb hovers over the accept button.

I don't know what she could want this late.

Find out, he suggests.
Money calling!

    Me: *Hello.*

Beth: *Hi, Jah-lyn. It's Beth.*

    Me: *Hi, Beth.*

Beth: *Sorry to call so late.*
Connor just said he can't come in Saturday,
but a new Disney movie premieres
this weekend. Can you cover him?

    Me: *Saturday?*

I sit up, forehead scrunched.
I have to be hearing her wrong.

Trey tries to catch my attention,
but I get on Google quickly,
search the premiere date, and hope
she's talking about next Saturday.

Beth: *Hello?*

    Me: *Sorry. This Saturday? What time?*

Beth: *Yes, from 7 to 11 p.m. But if you could come in even earlier, that would be great.*

I'm not missing the last night
of WestSide Roll for anything or anybody.
But I can't tell her that.

    Me: *Give me just a second.*

Trey reaches over and mutes
my phone.

    I need an excuse,
    I say.

You're going out of town.

    Please. Like that ever happens,
    I scoff.
    What if she finds out I lied?
    What if I don't get any more shifts?

Do any of your co-workers follow you on social media?

    No.

Do any of them skate?

    No.

Do you really need one, then?

    She barely schedules me as is.

*But you don't wanna miss
the last night, JJ.*

I stare at my phone,
contemplate telling the truth,
hoping that she'll understand
what the rink means to me.

Beth: *Are you there?*

I unmute the phone.

>Me: *Yes, sorry. I'm here.*
>*I won't be able to make it.*

She's quiet, waiting for an explanation   but I don't give her one.

ONE DAY UNTIL WESTSIDE ROLL CLOSES

Trey FaceTimes me, but I want to wallow today,
be by myself.

He hangs up, calls again,
keeping my screen busy.

Instead of switching my phone
to do not disturb, I answer.

His face is hidden in shadow.
The creases in his forehead are ripples.

> *Is everything okay?*
> I ask.

No. My parents are being so . . .
He lets out a breath
as he walks through his hallway.

He gets in his room,
shuts the door.
. . . Unreasonable.
I can't stand *them.*

I've never heard him talk about his parents,
assumed since they're still married
that it never got this bad for him.
That maybe they were like my parents before . . . everything.

What happened?

*They just trip off every. Little. Thing. I do.
Nothing is good enough for them.*

I nod, but he gets quiet.

Do you want to talk about it?

Not really, he says. *Can we hang out?*

Of course.

*Okay, I'm gonna head over.
Thanks, Jae.*

It's nothing.

I meet Trey at the door,

hands full with my purse,

a tote bag of snacks,

and a puffy camping blanket.

Before he can ask, I say,

*I was thinking we could go
to the lake. Since Betsy likes it so much.*

I like the way your mind works.

He smiles and grabs everything

out of my hands,

stuffs it under his arm

like a football,

grabs my hand with his free one.

1,400 acres of water,
3,900 of forest,
the Eagle Creek Reservoir
is the closest getaway we have.

The birds chirp   nestled in the trees thick with age.

The water is still   the grass bends with the breeze.

Me and Noe used to visit every year once spring hit.
We'd pack a picnic and stay for hours.

It's the opposite of WestSide Roll.
There, the loudness
and quickness of our wheels
help us de-stress.

But here
something about the calm
of the water sends our problems

                              swimming away.

Wanna hike before we set our stuff down?
I think you need to walk that anger out,
I say.

Don't remind me.
Trey forces a chuckle,
the first time I've heard him fake a laugh.

I lead us to a one-mile trail,
the same one I'd try to convince Noe to walk,
that blocks out every other sound in the city.

 So, what happened?
 I ask once we start on the trail.

Trey walks beside me,
towers over my frame,
can probably see so much more
from up there than I can.

I don't wanna talk about it yet.

 You can trust me.

I turn to stare at him,
but his face is stone, jaw sharp,
eyes staring straight ahead.
I see he takes his anger out on the world.

 Let's do some breathing exercises,
 I say, hoping my readings on healing
 will make this hike less intense.

 Deep breath in for four counts,
 hold it for four,
 let it all out for four.

As we walk?

Yeah, I say. *Walking meditation.*

We inhale together,
our noses sounding like waves against a seashore.
We hold the breath, our stroll slowing,
shoes scraping the almost-black soil.

We exhale and our arms brush against each other's.

Keep going,
I say before repeating.

These are the breaths
that taught me not to spiral
when my dad would text

then disappear for days   weeks   sometimes months.

These are the breaths
that gave me patience for my mama
when I thought she should have stopped
crying after the divorce.

Gave me patience for myself
because I was crying, too.

I couldn't stand my parents for a while, either,
I admit.

He cuts his inhale short.

Us
and the redbirds
and squirrels
are the trail's only company.

The trees shield us
and our worries from the rest of the world.

I would have never expected that.
Well, not with your mom.

> *I thought they were stupid for divorcing,*
> I say, and watch my shoes get dustier
> with each step.

What changed your mind?

> *I could tell they were both hurting and trying*
> *but couldn't find another solution.*

Hmm, Trey says, nodding.

We can see the lake now,
the gurgling growing louder.

Wow, Trey says, looking out
at the green-blue water.

I forgot you're new around here.
First time, right?

First time. Now you're putting me on.

I try. I smile.

We stand at the end of the trail
gazing at the water,
a few boats coasting through,
a mother duck leading her babies.

I don't know what to say to Trey.

He is a river dam,
only letting so much trickle out,
storing the rest behind a wall I can't tackle.

He tugs me by my hand,
brings me in close.

I stand in front of him, chin up to meet his eyes,
eyebrows drawing together in question.

Thank you for bringing me out here.
I needed it, he says.

He cracks a smile.
It vanishes
before I can revel in it.

You're welcome.

He pulls me into a hug.
I find my rightful place
on his chest

but I can't get comfortable in his grasp.

Ten

This is it. WestSide Roll's final night.

I lay my outfit on the bed,
black biker shorts
and a black crop top
so I can move freely.

My phone buzzes,
almost vibrating off the bed,
my dad's name on the screen.

Hey, lovebug. I know we haven't had the chance to talk
but since it's the last night, I'd love to skate with you.

This time he sends
"The Sweetest Taboo" by Sade,
a song he used to howl
when he hopped on the grill.

All of a sudden, I feel heavy.

If I tell him no, will I regret it?

My mama pops in my room
in booty shorts and a baggy V-neck tee,
hair slicked into a topknot.

How are you feeling?

> *Like I'm losing everything,* I say.
> I plop down on the bed
> opposite my outfit,
> swing my feet.

> *I can't believe it.*

Me neither, she says,
and sits next to me.

> *Nothing could have prepared me for tonight.*

It's devastating, my mama says.
Everybody I know out here,
I met at the rink.
Aside from Mrs. Joyce.

I nod.

Your dad will probably be there, she says.

> *I know. He already texted me.*

Saying what?

> *Asking to skate one last time,* I say.
> *I haven't decided.*

Before we leave, I snap a picture
of my reflection in the mirror
so I can have this moment forever.

So I can look at this photo and say,
this wasn't the day I lost the rink.

This was the day I chose to celebrate it.

For once, the radio station plays
all my, my mama's, and Noe's favorites
straight through with no commercials
as we head to the rink for the last Saturday ever.

But instead of Noe and me leaning into each other,
sharing our phone as mics to sing or rap into,
this time, we keep our faces committed
to our respective windows.

I keep thinking of all the lasts:
The last time I'll get ready for the rink in that apartment.
The last time we'll make this drive.
The last time me and Noe will sit in this back seat,
   anticipating a good night at WestSide Roll.

Mama lets us out by the WestSide Roll entrance,
says she'll find a parking spot.

I know y'all don't want me around,
so I'll be skating with the other oldheads.
Just text me if you need anything.

The line snakes around the building
like Beyoncé is inside.

We meet Trey in the back of the line,
and shortly after,
Kaila and Ashley join us.

You ready?
Trey asks me.

    Not at all.

I'll never be ready for this.
I've pictured it.
I've thought about my lonely Saturdays.
I've even searched Eventbrite for other things to do.

But nothing sounds as good.

Noe yanks me close, and says, *There's Nate.*

I'm curious about where Deon went,
who he was to begin with.

Before I can ask about Nate,
she pulls me in his direction,
pointing at him.

His locs brush his waist,
True Religion jeans still have the creases,
his shoes look fresh out the box.

After she introduces us,
she hangs all over him
like they're familiar.

They whisper to each other
as if they're sharing forbidden parts of themselves.

Then Noe turns to us,
smile so big it could rival
the sun, and says,

Nate thinks we should
get to the party
earlier than planned.

Typical, typical Noe.

I stare at the brick
of WestSide Roll,
trying to figure out
how to respond.

The painted purple script logo
is dark against the light brick,
and thick strokes of green and orange paint
embellish the front of the building.

> *What party?*
> *You know the rink is closing, right?*

Jae, you don't get it.
This is the *party of the summer.*
I told Kaila and Ashley earlier, and they're down,
she says in a whisper, and points to them
like I didn't know they were behind her.

Of course they're down.
If it has to do with Noe,
they're never not.

> *If it's the party of the summer,*
> *why didn't you mention it until now?*

We stare daggers at each other,
neither of us willing to lose.

I could have sworn I told you,
she says.

> *You didn't.*

My chest heaves
like a balloon
inflating and deflating.

Trey inches closer to me.
I inch closer to Noe.
We're almost face-to-face.

> *I'm not gonna miss out*
> *on this party because*
> *you have trouble letting things go.*

My body recoils without permission.

> *And I'm not about to miss out*
> *on the rink because you have to be seen*
> *at a party you didn't even*
> *tell your best friend about.*

I say it as soon as I think it,
voice louder than planned.
Heads turn to watch.

Nate keeps his arm wrapped around
Noe like I might snatch her.
Trey steps to my side,
ready to be a shield
for any foul words.

Then Noe is leaving and yells,

You have to get a life outside
of the rink because it's closing, okay?
It's not illegal to try something new.

Her words hit all my soft
and vulnerable targets.
I search her eyes for remorse.
Find none.

> *Noe, I am trying new things. I'm making friends,*
> *I have someone I really like. And you would know that*
> *if you paid any attention to me this summer.*

> *You don't care about anything but yourself,*
> *and you wonder why your life looks like it does.*

Everything
freezes
like a framed photo.

Me, standing slightly out of line,
burning with anger.

Noe, sandals stuck on the sidewalk like it's quicksand,
cheeks fire red, eyes searching for who I have become.

Wow, Jaelyn. Wow.

She starts walking again, not stuck at all,
trying to get as far away from me as possible.

We've never had a screaming match.
Our fights are silent—
Noe is loud in her avoidance,
I am so absent that I can be forgotten.

Noelle walks farther
         and   farther away.

I hope she'll turn around,
tell me that she's having a bad day.
Tell me she forgives the words I didn't mince.

I contemplate running toward her,
apologizing, asking her to stay.

Telling her I don't understand
how we became water and oil.

I think about calling her name,
admitting that it's not that I can't let go,

it's that everything I haven't
held on to with a tight grip has gone.

Trey stands beside me / I let / my head / ease onto his shoulder / rise / and fall / with Trey's body / we inch our way up / in line / me and Noe were so loud / angry / her words venom / breaking down / the softest parts of me / I should have told her / *I need you here* / but I was too / prideful / jealous / resentful / everything a best friend / shouldn't be / *Y'all are sisters* / *you'll fix things* / Trey says / but guilt / floods my body / I am / a natural / disaster

Once me and Trey are inside, I race to the lockers
like the rink will disappear any minute now.

I guess it really will.

I slip a quarter into a locker slot,
throw my shoes in, sit down to lace my skates.

When we get on the floor,
I tell Trey I need a moment.

After him being on guard yesterday at the lake,
I don't know where I stand with him.
But tonight isn't the night to figure it out.

Right now, I need to forget all the bad,
remember all the good.

My body sways left and right,
my feet cruise. Each muscle knows its role.
I wish life were this effortless.

DJ Sunny mixes in an upbeat song
and the oldheads start flying.

I soar with them, drift through all these skaters,
will my wheels to roll as hard as they can.

My knees bounce.
My calves keep me moving.

I weave in and out,
left and right.

I
can't
be
touched.

The problems
spill out of my body
and evaporate.

It's dizzying.

I raise one arm,
snap my fingers,
bop to the rhythm.

There are too many skaters
for me to close my eyes,
but I don't want to tonight.

I wanna see everybody
moving
grooving
loving

our brown skin
shimmering purples
and golds and greens
under the neon lights.

Skaters slide to the ground,
bust into splits, dribble or dip.

Mr. Mike swerves so hard his spine contorts.
It's his last night, too.
Of course he's on the rink floor with us
sharing the wood, commanding his wheels.

> I roll up to him.
> *Hey, Mr. Mike.*
> *How you doing?*

I'm doing, he says,
dabbing his head
with a sweat rag.

I get behind him,
throw my arm on his shoulder
and we roll together.

I replicate each twist, pivot, clap.

The bass pounds and rattles the walls,
skaters make a *clack!*
with their wheels
anytime they land a spin.

I know what you want to ask,
he says over his shoulder
once the song fades out.

He wipes his glistening head again
as we slow down.
Sweat has a home on his skin.

But there's nothing we can do.

I leave the skate floor defeated
even though I already knew
the answer to my question.

I wanted him to tell me
WestSide Roll could be saved.

That there's always a chance.

Can I have this skate?

my dad asks. I didn't even hear him
sit down at the bench next to me.

I don't know if you got my text earlier,
he adds, staring at his black skates,
the tongue exposing the shearling lining.

That's a pair you buy
when you're so serious about skating
that no dollar amount can deter you.
He's had them for years.

> *I did,*
> I say.

He nods.
Well, the offer is still on the table.

I consider it again.
I've already lost my chance to skate
with Noe at WestSide Roll one last time.

I won't miss out on skating with my dad,
even if I haven't forgiven him yet.

> *I'll take you up on the offer,*
> I say, a half smile rising from the left corner of my lips.

That means a lot, Jaelyn.

I still have so much to say, but now isn't the time.

Lead the way?

I ask.

I'll let you lead.

He places his right hand

on my shoulder

and we splice the crowd
with our moves

He mimics every step
keeps up with my flow

I remember when I learned
to skate this fast

I was so eager to show him
and one day he said, *Latch on*

then guided me through the rink
a proud grin on his face

Now I'm the one steering
us through traffic

Now he grips my shoulder tightly
like if he lets go

he'll lose me forever

I head to the Roller Café,
stand in line for nachos.

Trey sneaks up behind me.

> *Do you just watch me all night?*
> *Because how do you always know where I am?*

You want the honest answer?
he asks, cracking a smile.

Once we sit down,
he keeps staring.

His arms are open,
mine are folded.

He looks straight at me,
I watch the rink floor.

He grabs my hands to hold.
I accept.

> *I can't believe on the last night,*
> *Noe's not right next to me.*

The rink floor is full of friend duos arm in arm
or hand in hand, dragging each other
through the crowd like they're in a maze.

Trey gets up, comes to my side
of the table, sits close.

*He's playing all the songs
we used to love skating to together.*

I swear DJ Sunny has one of my and Noe's playlists,
bouncing from song to song
like tonight is a tribute to our friendship.

There's nothing I want to hear less.

All right, y'all, I wanna see backpacking
and some lovers on the floor.
This is your last night to shoot your shot.
Make it count,

DJ Sunny says as the lights lower
and a classic R&B jam starts.

Last backward skate?
Trey asks.

He stands up and extends his hand.
I examine his large palm,
the long heart line
deep as a valley.

Our lack of conversation at the lake replays in my head.
But I push the thoughts out and place my hand in his.

    Last backward skate.

Once we're on the floor,
we backpack—just what it sounds like,
his front to my back,
body to body.

Everyone skates slowly,
grinds the air or twists their legs
or moves their feet
out in out in like accordions.

Trey sings Keith Sweat's "Make It Last Forever,"
and I join in loudly.

Me and Noe used to sing this
at the top of our lungs anywhere.
We'd break out in song
at stores or restaurants
or during any quiet moment.

Maybe that's why I love music
so much on the skate floor.
Because there's always someone else
who feels it as deeply as you do.

Once the night is over,
we swarm the parking lot
like bees to a new hive.

Some still skate cause we ain't letting go tonight.

We'll always remember the rink's ugly carpet and scratched, shiny floor,
its nachos and Icees, its skate crews with matching shirts,
its broken lockers, its long lines.

Music oozes from cars loudly, like we're putting on
for WestSide Roll, trying to give to it
what it's given us all these years.

WestSide Roll won't come back, but we ain't letting go tonight.

Some folks guzzle beers,
pass vape pens,
laugh so loud it could be mistaken for yelling.

The crowded parking lot isn't ready to let go:
The oldheads with their thousand-dollar skates.
The skate crews forming circles and talking.
The skaters my age recording and taking pictures.
The nonskaters who just want to pay respects.
Not one of us, even the newcomers, is ready.

This feels like the first time
I got dropped off without supervision.
Something buzzes inside of me
as we fill the air with joy.

Eleven

FIVE DAYS SINCE WESTSIDE ROLL CLOSED

Trey knocks on my front door
instead of texting
because he swears
he likes to be old-school.

I give myself a once-over in the mirror,
fluff my curly hair with my fingers,
make sure my tour tee and biker shorts
give cute but relaxed.

I rush to the hall closet, grab my socks and skates,
slip on my sandals at the front door and swing it open.

    Hey, I say.

The light behind him makes his body glow like a halo.
We have an hour before the sun completely sets.

Hey.
He looks down at my skates.
I thought you said we were walking.

I invited him to take a walk
because I am bored,
restless,
losing it.

But really, Tiana told me that Deon's neighborhood
has a tennis court. Apparently, it's run-down now.
But it's there. A place to skate.

> *We are. Grab your skates*
> *from your car.*

I didn't bring any socks.

> *What skater drives around with skates*
> *but no socks?* I ask.

An amateur like me.

> *You have a point.*
> *Hold on.*

I go find a pair that isn't mine,
stolen from the laundromat on accident.
I return to the door,
hand them to him.

He frowns.
Man, whose socks are these?

> *I couldn't tell you.*

We start out on our walk
and Trey's face quizzes me
but I ignore it.

I haven't walked around here lately.

Last summer,
we could walk
to the beauty supply
or the vinyl shop.

We're running out of things to walk to.

If me and Noe got bored,
we'd walk around the complex,
share stories we've told a million times
like it's new news.

Walking was our ritual
and now we can barely stand being near each other.

Now, maybe, it'll become
mine and Tiana's.

Trey reaches for my hand.
I let mine settle in his.

We round the corner
out of my complex
and into the subdivision nearby.

Some of the ranch houses
need new paint jobs,
have moss crawling up their sides.

Bikes are deserted on the sidewalks,
abandoned chalk cracked and scattered,
residue blueing the pavement.

Do you know people over here?
Trey asks.

    Only a guy named Deon that Noe was messing with.

We pass house after house,
an open garage with a man smoking a Black & Mild to our right,
someone fixing a car in the driveway to our left.

    Do you know people where you live?

He chuckles.
Not really. I don't like it.

    Why?

It's not that far from you, but it's so different.
Most of the houses look like that.

He points across the street
to a black two-story home,
boxy like a refrigerator,
chimney stacked on top
like a failed game of Tetris.

I can't stop staring
between that house
and the one next to it,

half its height,
drowning in shadows
that the new home casts.

Does your place look like that?

No, but it seems like every home near me
is being renovated like this.
They're all owned by the same company.

I cross the street to get a closer look
at the yard sign that reads

LIVINGSTON HOMES:
YOUR LUXURY AWAITS.

Nothing about neglected homes,
landlords who don't care,
and potholes that will kill a tire
scream *luxury* to me.

Trey stands behind me,
tapping at his screen.

*Apparently, they're building
a few more houses in this area,*
he says.

    I bet they are.

I keep walking,
rushing this time,
trying to avoid
seeing anything else

that tells me the West Side isn't ours anymore.

Trey follows me through the park's half-dead grass
and into the gate.

We swivel around to inspect the weathered court.
There's only enough space for one pair to play tennis.
The net is missing like it was torn off.

> *From what I've seen on social media,*
> *skaters who don't have a rink nearby*
> *go to a tennis court instead.*
>
> *Smoother than a street, close enough*
> *to hardwood, I guess?*

Makes sense.

Trey leans against the black gate
to put his skates on.

His fingers move against the laces
slow, gentle, almost caressing them.
He takes his time, hands steady.

I stand next to him, connecting
my portable speaker to my phone.

This is a good idea, JJ,
he says.

I try, I try, I say.

I lace my skates up quicker than him,
notice my pink laces have a grayish hue,
inspect all the scuffs and nicks WestSide Roll birthed.

I made a skate routine for you
of all the things you've taught me so far,
Trey says over the music.
Which isn't much. You're not the best teacher.

I shake my head.
He's both cute and outlandish.

But you've inspired me to skate on my own.
I be out in those suburbs
trying to spin like my life depends on it.

    And I haven't seen these moves?

You're about to!
He smirks and winks.

Trey starts gliding, acquainting himself
with smooth. He crosses his feet,
spins, skates closer to me
then away, arms pan to the left and right.

He sings along,
deep voice cracking as he attempts
to serenade and skate at the same time.

He comes back toward me,
breathless, face radiant
like all the lights in town
are erupting from his body.

Skate with me.

I nestle into him.
He holds my waist,
and when I lean against him,
I feel his heartbeat.

For once, I follow Trey's lead.
Like water, we bend to each other.
His backward skate is careful
but he's found his style

and his arms
won't let me
fall.

You wanna watch the stars? I ask
after we've skated to half of my playlist.

We unlace our skates,
gently pull them from our feet,
and place them near our shoes.

Trey lies down,
hands behind his head,
chest open for me to lie on.
I snuggle into the warmth of him.

Look at that,
he says, pointing
up at a cluster.

They're bright,
full of fire, so close
we could pluck them.

They remind me of you.
Every time something gets you down,
you get back up and shine.

Is that right?

Yeah. I mean, even with the rink.
It just closed and you're already
trying to recreate it.

He leans over, pecks
me on the forehead softly.

> *Confident Trey, admiring*
> *someone else that much?*

Truest thing that's ever
left my mouth.

> *So you be lying?*

You're ruining the moment,
he says, and laughs.

I get quiet and kiss his cheek.

> *Thank you,* I say. *You're the same way.*

He sighs heavily.

> *Am I wrong?*
> *What am I missing?*

Nothing.

> *Tell me.*

A plane soars through the navy blue sky,
leaving two streaks behind.

I don't think
anyone I used to know
would see it that way.

> *What happened over there?*
> *You've been weird*
> *about it since we've met.*
> *That's the only thing*
> *you're not open about.*

I pause.

> *You know my whole life.*
> *I want to know yours.*

He turns to catch my eyes.
I search his for what they're hiding.

> *Trey.*

I hate begging him to open up.
I hate having to force
what I believe I've earned.

His inhale sucks up all the air.
His sigh becomes the wind,
tickles the grass outside the court.

> *Do you not trust me?*

I don't trust anyone,
he says.

The hurt of this truth
shocks me straight up
from my lying position,
destroys what I thought I knew.

What I thought we had.

> *I've been nothing*
> *but honest with you,*
> I squeak out.

It's not you.

> *Well, what is it?*
> *Do I not deserve to know?*

My words are so tight
they squish together.

He doesn't answer.

> *Fine, forget it, then.*
> *Act like I never asked.*

I fold my arms across
my chest, hug myself.

Minutes go by.
Part of me wants to leave,
part of me knows that we should have
had this conversation before today.

Okay, you're right.
You do deserve to know.

I roll my eyes,
hear the *but I don't want to tell you*
that he doesn't say.

I got expelled from my last school.
Trey refuses to look in my direction,
keeps his eyes locked on the stars.

It takes everything in me not to gasp.

I got caught with a knife.
Well, two.
And they have a zero-tolerance policy for weapons.

His voice is almost a whisper,
the rumble of his throat
the only thing giving his words bass.

    Trey, what?

Not for anything violent.

    Okay . . .

It's a long story.

    Well?

I have this thing I do.
And it's embarrassing.

I never wanted to tell you.
I thought if we skated enough,
I wouldn't have a reason to.

He takes a beat.

I give him space to keep going.
If I interrupt, I know he'll stop completely.

I'm not that good at school.
So sometimes, if class got too hard, I'd go to the pool,
hide behind the bleachers, and shut it all out.

What's the thing?

You're going to think I'm weird.

I promise I'll never think you're weird.

He sits up, faces me.

I build model cars. Okay?
His words rush out,
brows knit together.

I consider what it means to enjoy playing with knives,
to love the sharpness of a thing,
to cradle it like something soft,

safe.

I always notice how	**careful his hands are**
where I am clumsy	he is still, stable
where I rush	he moves at his own tempo
lacing his skates	changing the song while he's driving
caressing my face	tapping his fingers to a dance-worthy beat

Why were you scared to tell me that?

I stare into his eyes, still and dull.
Lacking his usual twinkle.

It's embarrassing.

    Says who?

Me,
he says,
chest puffed out.

The wind switches direction,
blows my hair back and reveals my face,
my curls no longer obstructing his view.

    I'm so sorry, Trey.
    Is this why you moved?

When he speaks, it's shaky.

Not even two weeks
after me and my ex-girlfriend broke up,
somebody snitched me out.

Administration checked my body,
my locker, all my stuff,
said somebody told them
I was dangerous.

He pauses again,
swallows the lump in his throat.

It's so wild because she told me
she loved me but never once
                         admitted
she played a part.

Ever since, I've been the son my parents have to watch.
They have an image to uphold and
a troublemaking son isn't part of that.

I reach out, rub his cheek with my thumb.

    I appreciate you sharing that with me.
    I just don't get why you didn't tell me sooner.

I didn't want to talk about it, Jaelyn.

He reverts to my full name
like we're new to each other.

    That's not fair.

It is. This is what I have to deal with.
I lost everything I knew.

    And I know what that feels like.

But your family still loves you and you still have friends.

I want so badly to be here for him,
to tell him that none of this makes him a bad person,
but he doesn't want to hear it.
He doesn't want my comfort.

    I'm gonna go, I say,

peeling myself
from the ground,

sulking out of the tennis court,
and heading home

                              alone.

Twelve

TEN DAYS SINCE WESTSIDE ROLL CLOSED

My next morning off from work, I grab a lawn chair
and take it to Mrs. Joyce's
before any kids are outside
throwing objects in my direction.

The breeze is soft.
Not too warm but welcoming,
telling me to sit awhile.

Good morning, Granny,
I say when she opens the door.

Good morning, baby.
Nice day out here, isn't it?
Let me get my chair.

She walks inside slower than usual,
then sets her chair next to mine.
I go in to grab our usual lemonades.

Mrs. Joyce cautiously sits
and it takes a while for her to land in the seat.
She sips her lemonade and looks off into the distance.

I feel Granny's eyes on me.

What ya thinking about?
She places her cup to her lips and drinks.

My mama attempts to make her lemonade the same way
but fails. Sometimes too bitter, sometimes too sweet.

What am I not thinking about is the better question.

Stop with the riddles.
What's on your mind?

I sigh.
Mrs. Joyce can always sense my frustration.

I feel like I've lost so much
and can't do anything about it.

Well, that's not true.

How isn't it?
The rink just closed.
I couldn't keep me and Noe—

I stop. Even though she's family, too,
I try to shield her from problems with Noe.

You two will make up.

Who said we weren't up?
I crack a smile.

~ 227 ~

I ain't stupid.

Her breaths are labored,
though we haven't moved.
She rubs her chest with her fingertips.

Are you okay?

I'm fine. Allergies.

Anyway, you might not be able
to stop anything,
but you can always control
how you make up for what's lost.

Maybe. But it won't be the same.

Should it be? If everything in my life
remained the same, you wouldn't be sitting here.
Noelle wouldn't be in my care.
You two wouldn't have met.

Change is an opportunity.

The sweet cold sting of lemonade slides down my throat.

She makes it sound so easy
but at every turn,
change has flipped my life on its head.

Skating at the tennis court
was the newest thing I've tried

but it feels like I'm chasing
something that doesn't exist anymore.

And what's this about this boy
you've been running around with?

> Dang, Granny. All up in my business.

Your business is my business.

> I think you'd like him.

Debatable.
She laughs and I join her.

Mrs. Joyce likes everybody
except the boys she hears
me and Noe hang around.

> *He's smart, funny, charming. Talkative.*

But?

> *But he just told me*
> *about getting in trouble*
> *at his last school. And I wish he would*
> *have told me sooner.*
> *He doesn't trust me.*

A fly skitters around us like it's part of the conversation.

Did you do something to lose his trust?

No. Someone from his past did.

You gotta give him time.
He don't know you from a can of paint.

We do know each other.

Jaelyn, give the boy time.
If he's holding back, there's a reason.

Her neighbor Dominique opens her screen door.

Hey, Mrs. Joyce and Jaelyn!
she says as her twins rip into the yard.

I wave. Mrs. Joyce says,
Hey, honey, how are you?

I'm all right.
Are you free to watch them for a few?
I gotta make some phone calls.

Of course,
Granny says between more thick breaths.
I watch her chest rise and fall as she tries to control them.

I don't dare demand to know what's wrong.
But I notice the new crease in Granny's forehead,
how her back has curved forward.

She's nearing eighty, doesn't move the same.

She used to sing and dance right along with my mama,

used to say she was a young seventysomething.

Dominique thanks her,

leaves us to watch the twins play tag.

A white man in a suit approaches,
stack of papers in hand thick as a mattress,
two cops behind him.

Can we help you? Mrs. Joyce asks,
swirls her lemonade so the cubes clink.
Her raised eyebrow tells me she's tucking words away.

He hands both of us a sheet
from his stack, still warm,
fresh off the printer. It reads:

RENT INCREASE NOTICE

This letter is to inform you that effective upon lease renewal,

the new rates will be as follows:

1-BR from $775 to $1,216

2-BR from $905 to $1,521

3-BR from $1,312 to $1,788

Additionally, no rental-assistance programs will be accepted.

Any resident who does not wish to renew, we ask that you give us

proper thirty days' notice to vacate in writing.

As always, we thank you for your continued residency.

Mrs. Joyce gets up,
folds her chair.
Malik and Malia,
come on inside with us for a bit.

The paper trembles in my hand.

I read it to myself

again,

    try to

        rearrange

    the words.

When me and my mama moved here,
I thought it needed fixing.
But I learned it's valuable because of what it is,
not what it can become.

Because all of us here hold each other down,
buy each other's lemonade,
watch each other's packages,
offer each other food,
trust each other to babysit.

Nothing like what I experienced in Plainfield.
Maybe the neighbors did that for each other,
but they never did it for us.

                                    Instead of helping us stay,
            these developers want to push   us out,
                             price everything just
                  outside

                                        of our reach,
                                      our possibility.

                        We could have protested for days,
                        filled the highways with our bodies,
                        and they still would have told us

                              to move out of the way
                              so they can move on in.

I watch the wall clock

above my dining room table,

count the minutes

until my mama walks through the door

I debated about warning her

before she got home

The texts I erased said:

hey mama, we just got news from the complex

or hey, there's something important for you on the table when you get home

or the rent is going up once we renew our lease

or i think we'll have to move

or [attached photo]

None of them felt right

so I tucked my phone away

And I still don't know how

to hand her a paper

that will change our entire year

She bursts in like gushing water,
flows into the kitchen,
probably on the phone with my auntie.

Says, *Girl, they done pissed me off today.*

I contemplate
snatching the paper
from the table.

I contemplate hiding it,
waiting for a better moment,
but there's no better moment
to tell my mama that the rent is hundreds more.

She slams the fridge,
fills a cup with something,
opens the fridge,
slams it again.

I was about to lose my job today.

My mama rushes into the dining room,
uses the back of one of the chairs
as a purse hanger,
slams her cup on the table.

Water sloshes out.

She sheds her jacket,
alternates ears with her phone.

Okay, I'll let you go.
I need to relax.
She tells whoever.

When she hangs up,
she starts again.

You won't believe what happened at work today.

Then she goes on,
sailing through the living room,
folding our blankets as she tells me

how someone cussed her out
because they got scammed out of $30.
How someone else told her she's a dummy
and shouldn't work at a bank.

I'm getting too old for this,
she says, diving onto the couch
in her work uniform.
She points the remote to the TV.

                      I say,
          Mama, something from the complex
                came for us today.

Hand it to me,
she says.

I grab the paper,
wondering if I should issue a warning
or wait for her to detonate after reading.

It's about the rent,
I mumble as I hand it to her.

Her eyes scan the paper,
squinted, like there's something missing.

Un-fucking-believable,
she says as she rises from the couch,
paper still in hand.

When did they give this to you?
she asks, facing me.

Un-fucking-believable!
she shouts before I can answer.
My mama stomps into the dining room,
grabs her keys.

They jingle as she talks,
her hands jerking every which way.

This don't make no sense.
We have six months until our rent goes up?
We have six months to either find the money
or a new apartment?
Un-fucking-believable.

Anything I say
won't make this better
but I try.

We're gonna figure it out, Mama.

*Everybody in that leasing office
is about to figure something out.*

My mama storms out,
keys gripped so tightly
that they don't make a sound.

Thirteen

FOURTEEN DAYS SINCE WESTSIDE ROLL CLOSED

It's Monday and no matter how far back
my skates are tucked in the hall closet,
the feeling that I'll pull them out
for Thursday Skate and Saturday Skate
is as present as mama's quiet rage about the rent.

I search for the nearest rink
and realize it's near my old neighborhood.
I figure I'll go alone,
release what's steeping inside of me.

The tennis court is okay
but there's nothing like a wooden floor,
a DJ pumping music,
and people around you
who love their eight wheels
more than anything.

Even the feeling

at the entrance of Avon Roller Rink

                    is different.

No one chilling

                    outside.

No Mr. Mike peering

                    through the glass

to see who's coming.

I'm met with printed rules

                    taped down at least ten times

to the door.

The rules, all nineteen of them:

1. Parent or guardian spectators only.
2. No outside food or drinks in the building.
3. Dress code is strictly enforced: No hats, sagging pants, coats, men's tank tops, jackets, bandannas, ball caps, or backpacks are to be worn inside the building. All bags are subject to inspection.
4. No cell phones or earphones while skating.
5. No in-and-out privileges.
6. All skates must be clean and safe. If you do not have stops or plugs, you cannot skate.
7. Profanity and negative slang are prohibited.
8. No refunds or exchanges.
9. Management may revoke entry at any time.
10. Follow roller skating etiquette. Fast skating, trick skating, and disruptive skating are not allowed. No horseplay on the rink floor.
11. Gambling is strictly prohibited.
12. Sexual dancing, sexual conduct, or other inappropriate behavior is not permitted.
13. No fighting of any kind. You will be banned from the premises.
14. We do not allow anyone to possess alcohol, nonprescribed drugs, illegal substances, or any other substances. If we believe you are under the influence of any substance, you will be asked to leave.
15. Harassment will not be tolerated.
16. No gum chewing while skating.
17. No weapons permitted.
18. No one is allowed to sit on the skating floor.
19. Pregnant women are not allowed to skate.

What the rules tell me:

I walk in anyway

and hand the cashier,

my age and brunette,

my debit card.

The rink doesn't have the scent

of sweat or nacho cheese or socks.

It's like no one visits,

and if they do, they don't stay long.

The cashier doesn't greet me.

The music isn't loud.

There's no DJ booth on the floor.

There's not a Black employee in sight.

She wraps a blue wristband

around my arm tight

like cuffs.

I shift my skates

from one arm to the other

and walk toward the lockers.

They're bright orange,

situated differently than WestSide Roll,

aligned against the farthest wall

instead of cramped in one area.

I find a place to sit

and lace my skates up,

Lana Del Rey playing at nearly a whisper.

I roll onto the hardwood without caution.

There are four skaters here, myself included.

Of us, two are skating so slowly that I know a fall is coming.

I slide my wireless headphones out of my pocket,
insert both, let my coils cover my ears.

Some oldheads at WestSide Roll did this
whenever new rap and R&B played.
They just needed access to a floor.

I start my neo-soul playlist,
attempt to move my body like I used to.

I fling myself into movement,
let gravity control me, shimmy to the rhythm.
I want to shake off everything.

The closing.
The arguments.
The rent increase.

I want to shake off all the tears I've cried
and all the ones I probably will.

I want to shake off the rules
that I will disobey just by being.

I want to shake off wanting Noe here.

I want to shake off everything Trey said
and everything he didn't.

The music courses through me like blood.

I feel each lyric in my toes,

fingertips, up and down my spine.

But when I open my eyes

everyone on the skate floor

is watching me

bewildered.

Someone on a mic

warns me to slow down, and then,

No tricks. No tricks.

I've only done a spin or two.

I'm not gonna let this rink steal

what little joy I have left.

I turn down my headphones

in case someone gets on the mic again.

But now my vibe is ruined,

body stubborn.

I thought I could skate anywhere

as long as I had wheels

and good music.

But I have both

(at least in my headphones)

and it's still not enough.

I leave the rink floor

as easy as I arrived,

take off my skates,
slip on my sandals,
tear the wristband off,
and walk out the door.

Hey, baby girl.

My dad texts as soon as I'm outside.

I'm glad we got to skate. I was hoping we could spend some time together soon?

Once I'm outside
I type
Okay

Delete.

I type
Maybe

Delete.

I type
Why now?

Delete.

He sends another.

I'm willing to be patient. I just want you to know that you are my #1 priority from now on.

I type
That should have always been the case

Delete.

~ 249 ~

I finally respond
Let me think about it

and request an Uber.

You know your drop-off is permanently closed, right?
my driver asks as he pulls off.

I know.

He stares at me curiously
through the rearview mirror,
then focuses on the road again.

We pass homes in Plainfield with
two- or three-car garages,
two or three stories,
manicured lawns,
straight out of HGTV.

The grass isn't patchy,
sidewalks aren't stained,
they're absent of litter.

It's as pristine as it was when we moved.

I thank the driver
before getting out of the car
and standing on the curb.

Every sign and flyer
that decked out the front door
of WestSide Roll is gone,
tape residue scraped away.

The painted purple script logo
and background colors
still embellish the front of the building.
I walk to the entrance,
peek into the dark emptiness.

The arcade games,
glass display for prizes,
lockers, rental skates, gone.

I thought coming here would make me feel at home,
but this is like the closing announcement all over again.

My fists tighten.
My teeth grind like the top row
is sanding the bottom.

Mrs. Joyce says the violence
of gentrification is usually silent.
It starts with paving the streets and potholes
that we've complained about for years.

Then comes the jogging.

The quiet pitter-patter of running shoes.

The sneers as runners approach
the convenience store or gas station
we've always relied on.

It's sneaky.
It waits,
stalks its prey,
attacks

when our minds are elsewhere.

I take my phone out of my pocket,
raise it to the building and parking lot,
capture a photo of the small changes.

I start to share it with Trey,
then remember
we haven't talked much.

Not because of him,
but because of me.

He'll ask, Hey, how's your day,
and my responses are short—
It's fine or It's going.

Can we talk?

he'll ask,

and just like my text thread with my dad,

I'll type delete type delete

until I decide to say nothing.

Fourteen

NINETEEN DAYS SINCE WESTSIDE ROLL CLOSED

I walk into work / red polo tucked / into black slacks / badge pinned / on my shirt / like I am property / I haven't been scheduled / for weeks / or haven't been / scheduled / enough / I need hours / because no / our lease isn't over / until winter / but yes / I will have to help / financially / even though my mama / told me not to worry / that she's handling it / and even though / it's months away / my stomach / chest / aches / feels like it's / cracking / like an egg / leaving me / runny yolk / I plaster on / a pageant smile / march through / the doors.

Beth has a frown etched on her face.

Fancy seeing you here,
she says, like I create my own hours.

    Fancy being on the schedule,
    I say, turning my back to clock in at the station.

I told her no weeks ago, now the most
I get scheduled is four hours a week.
I'm legally allowed to work thirty during the summer.

She looms behind me.
My body heats
from what I just let
slip
out of my typically passive mouth.

Our daily assignment bulletin board
says I'm on cleanup duty
for theaters six through nine,

sweeping popcorn
and catching drink spills
before they're sticky like putty.

    Beth?
    I ask, my back to her
    standing at the employee room's door.

Yes, Jaelyn?

She mispronounces my name again.

I'm sick of it.

Sick of it.

Fucking sick.

I roll my shoulders back.

It's Jay-lyn. Jay. Lyn.

That's what I said.

She continues to shuffle through papers
like she's looking for something.

I was hired for fifteen to twenty hours a week.
Why haven't I been on the schedule?

The clock
above the bulletin board

ticks

                ticks.

Her shuffling

                halts.

I can tell she's thinking of an answer.
Ever since she replaced my last boss,
a Black woman, I've been ignored,
talked down to,
scheduled less.

When management looked like me,
I never had worry weighing on my chest
like a barbell.

> Should I look for another job?
> I ask because she's taking her sweet time.

After tonight,
that might be best.

Her eyes pierce my insides.
Anger rumbles in me.
My heart pumps, its rhythm so strong
my ears are beating.

I should have known that no hours
means practically no job.

That things would change here
like they have everywhere else on the West Side.

That she was searching for a reason
and I handed it to her.

> How about I start looking now?

I remove my badge,
place it on the counter next to me,
and walk out.

I weave through the customers
    in the lobby.
        My vision set
            on the door that will free me.

        With every step
        I question
        what I'll do next,
        if I should turn around,
        beg for my job back.

But once I emerge
from the automatic doors

my hands loosen.

I feel so relieved
I could run all the way home.

I walk eight blocks,
sweaty as a melting Popsicle.
Adrenaline rushes through me
like a car through a yellow light.

I pass a plaza half full
with businesses, the others displaying
For Sale signs in the dirty windows.

I pass the mall,
shoppers bombarding the entrance
for new stores we can't afford.

The more I walk,
I am reminded
that Beth is a newcomer
who wants me to believe I no longer belong.

Somebody, a few somebodies,
want us to believe
this neighborhood isn't ours anymore.

But it will always be.

No matter what we lose

                                    it is

    ours   ours   ours.

                    And no one can steal that.

I FaceTime my mama when I'm five minutes
from home so I don't startle her
with my sweat and panting
and tears prickling, which I didn't notice at first.

Hello? You okay?
my mama asks,
her camera pointing toward her bedroom ceiling.

I blink away
the wetness.

>*I'm sorry, Mama.*

Sorry for what?
She leans into the phone,
confusion taking control
of her expression.

>*I quit. Beth made me so mad*
>*and she hasn't been giving me hours*
>*so I quit on the spot.*
>*I know you say give two weeks but I couldn't.*
>*She didn't want me there from th—*

Jaelyn, Jaelyn. Slow down.
My mama's voice is mellow
but urgent, calming my spiral.

Why are you apologizing?

Because I know that my checks help.

She shuts her eyes gently,
shakes her head.

I'm *sorry*, she says.
*You're sixteen. You shouldn't be panicked
because of money. I told you I'm figuring out
our living situation. This is not your worry to carry.*

She sighs.
We'll talk when you get home, okay?

We say our goodbyes.

I've been holding everything in,
letting words get stuck in my throat,
letting anger / sadness / resentment
rest in me.

I won't do it anymore.
I can't
if I want

the kind of free
that skating makes me.

Fifteen

TWENTY-ONE DAYS SINCE WESTSIDE ROLL CLOSED

I need my best friend.
So I'm at Steak 'n Shake for lunch
to pick up her fave:

a frisco melt, garlic fries, strawberry-banana shake.

My plan might not work—an apology,
her favorite meal, a truce.
But I've had enough
of not seeing her,

not being able to share
my life with her.
Going through so much
without her friendship.

When I get to her apartment, I knock and knock
until she finally opens. Hair in a messy bun,
robe on, old acrylic nails lifting.

Can I come in? I ask through the screen.

Noe rolls her eyes, flicks the screen lock,
walks into the living room's gloom.
I step in, eyes adjusting.

~ 263 ~

How are you?

No answer.

I trail behind her to the kitchen,
watch her fill a glass   half empty,
then follow her to Granny's room.

Stay here, she says,
even though I usually
at least let Granny know that I'm here.

She returns and I follow her to her room.

    I got your favorite, I say, holding up
    the greasy paper bag, hoping it'll get me answers.

She lets out a sigh as big as the place
when she lies down on her bed.

I'm still mad at you, she says,
staring at a blank spot on the wall.

    I know.
    I'm still mad at you.

Tears well but she's not a crier.
I want to comfort her like my mama does me,
grab her up and tell her things will work themselves out.

But I'm scared to even approach.
I'm scared we're broken,
little shards of glass smashed and scattered
that I don't want to get cut by.

Granny isn't okay,
she whispers.

Suddenly
I feel like I've fallen.
No air in my lungs.
Limbs heavy and heart thumping.

I noticed Granny was different but never wanted to ask.
Never wanted my suspicions to be real.

    What's going on?
    I ask.

It's her blood pressure.

She curls up in my lap   then shudders.
The tears fall   quietly
the way
a small stream flows.

Once she sits up,
I grab a Kleenex
from her vanity
and wipe her eyes.

Why didn't you tell me? What's wrong?

It's higher than it's ever been and she fainted.
She didn't want you to worry. It was Granny's decision.

I don't know anything about high blood pressure.
What it means for a woman her age.
Worry consumes me.

Noe gets up to bring the Kleenex box to the bed.

That's also why I was with Kaila and Ashley so much.
Kaila lives with her grandma, too.
She just gets things that you don't have to worry about yet.

I let it sink in. I never thought
about what living with Granny was like.

My mama is healthy, rarely sick,
but Granny has had high blood pressure
as long as I've known her.

And has managed it, so I thought.

Noe falls back,
lets her head hit the pillow.
I rest next to her.

Her eyes are locked
on the dark spot on the ceiling,
brown spreading, disrupting the white.
She's probably stared at it for days.

> *So you told them?*

*Granny had a scare
while we were practicing
at Ashley's and I had to run out.*

> *I wish you would have told me.
> I've been so deep in my own shit
> that I haven't looked up from it
> to see yours. I'm so sorry, Noe,* I say.

It's not your fault.

> *About our argument, too.*

> *I should have never said those things.
> I wanted to hurt you as much as you hurt me.
> I wanted you to hear me and show up for me
> the way I've needed you to all summer.
> But I never should have talked to you like that.*

She sniffles, stares at that spot again.

I forgive you, she says.
And I'm sorry, too.

I have so much going on,
I wanted to feel good.
I needed distractions outside of the rink.
Kaila and Ashley are always ready to try or do something.

I know you loved WestSide Roll,
but I only went because you did.
I should have told you.

I never asked why she went but didn't always skate.

I never assumed it was only for me.
I always thought she enjoyed dancing,
meeting people,
the vibes.

I reach out to hug her.
We hold each other tighter
than pinkies in a promise.

It's the first hug we've shared in weeks.

We finally open the food,
the fries soggy, inedible.

But she doesn't seem to notice,
passes me my order and scarfs down hers.

I can tell she hasn't eaten much,
Granny has been the priority.

> *What are you and Granny gonna do*
> *about the notice we got?*
> *If she's even been able to think about it,*
> I ask.

She said we'll have to find an apartment
that accepts Section 8. I can't believe this is legal.

> *It shouldn't be. We've been living here so long.*
> *If we need to call around, you know we will help.*

Thanks, Jae. I can't let her do this on her own.

Noe scrolls through streaming services
and I know she's looking for our movie,
The Best Man.

The first time we saw it,
my mama kept saying, *This is a classic.*
We covered our eyes during the sex scenes,
giggled about the curse words.

Me and Noe usually start with the original,
then run through the sequels,
always deciding which character is the messiest,
who we're in love with, which one is the type of guy we want
and which one isn't.

And each time, gush about Morris Chestnut.

She'll say,
I want a love like that,
when characters are soft
with each other.

>I'll say,
>*I hope we find it.*

Once I make it home

my mama is in the kitchen.

> *It smells good in here,*
> I say.

Smothered chicken,
she responds, pulling open
the oven door and peering in.
It should be done in about fifteen.

I watch her move through the kitchen,
from the sink to the pot of rice on the stove
to the salad on the counter she tosses a few times.

> *Did you know Granny fainted?*
> I ask.

She stops in her tracks,
takes a deep breath.

I did.

I jerk back.
Why am I the last to know?

> *Why didn't you tell me?*

Mrs. Joyce wanted to tell you herself.
Which I'm guessing she did.

No, she didn't.

Noe told me.

Were you ever going to?

I wanted to respect her decision, Jaelyn.

She turns the burner off
and removes the rice from the heat.

Sometimes you have to let people come to you,
my mama says.

I try to push down the hurt.

I hear her,
but I shouldn't have been the only one in the dark.
Me and Mrs. Joyce spend enough time together.
I didn't know I should have offered more help.

Can you put my plate
in the microwave? I'll eat later.

Jaelyn, come on.

I'm not hungry. I just need to think.

Before she puts up more of a fight, I go to my room.

I drop my purse,
jacket,
switch into my pajamas.

I lie in bed
and find a playlist
that will drown out all these feelings.

Tiana texts as I'm listening.

Tiana: Wyd tomorrow night?

Me: Nothing wassup?

Tiana: Mook is having a basement skate. He said pull up.

I can't forget that every time I've skated
since WestSide Roll closed
it hasn't been the same.

Me: Nah I just feel like chilling

Tiana: Okay well let me know if you change your mind

The R&B continues, each note embracing me.
But louder than that is Mrs. Joyce's voice echoing,

You might not be able to stop anything,
but you can always control
how you make up for what's lost.

Me: Actually, let me get out the house

Tiana: Okay lmk when you're ready tomorrow
and I'll come get you

Sixteen

TWENTY-TWO DAYS SINCE WESTSIDE ROLL CLOSED

I swear the house quivers
from the basement music bouncing
when we pull up.

That tingle,
that spark
I used to get
when I got out the car
at WestSide Roll,
slithers through me.

Mook commands

the middle of the basement.

It's tight in here,
square with a low ceiling.
The floor is wooden,
the fancy kind that isn't authentic.

But the LED lights make us feel like we're elsewhere.

Me, Tiana, Lailani,
and five other skaters I don't know
circle around Mook
like a dance battle.

He's only competing with himself,
footwork matching
the 1, 2, 3, 1, 2, 3
of the melody.

Our bodies rock
side to side
as our eyes follow
his every movement.

Mook is like a figure skater,
his body graceful
as he takes up every part
of the circle we've made for him.

His locs hide his eyebrows,
eyes,
but he never missteps.

He eventually yields the circle,
finds a spot within the crowd.

"Square Biz" by Teena Marie comes on
and I glide into the middle.

I'm transported back to WestSide Roll.
I shuffle side to side
as the horns have their moment.

Once Teena starts singing
I burst into movement,

begin with crazy legs,
knees bent,
feet shaking.

I lower myself,
turn turn turn
like a spin top.

Okay, Jaeeee,
Tiana shouts over the music.

The entire circle claps to the beat
as I let myself slip
into each move.

My feet take me where they want to go.
My eyes are shut tight.
I'm aware of the space I have
and I use it.

I twist, sing like I'm alone in my room.

This is the first song
I remember skating to
once I finally got good.

I try footwork like Mook's,
knot my feet up
and release them.

I try to float like Tiana,
lift a leg like a cheerleader
and coast across the room.

This circle is mine.
It is everything
I've been wanting.

As the song ends,
I open my eyes
and stare right into Trey's.

Those beautiful brown portals
that I can never resist.

He's dressed simply today—
black tee, thin gold chain,
black jeans.

The pang in my heart halts me completely.
I stand in the middle of the circle
as everyone applauds my freestyle.

I miss him.

I miss the way he clings onto me
when we're skating
and when we're completely still.

I miss the way he rubs his hand
across his neck when he's nervous or thinking.

I miss the passion of his kisses.

Before I can skate away
he skates toward me.
My wheels are glued to the floor.

Hey. He gives me a half smile.

   Hey.

Can we talk?

I can't do anything but nod,
my lips refuse to move.

I have so much to say
that my brain scrambles all the words
and nothing comes out.

I follow him up the basement stairs,
holding the banister tight.
He stops in the kitchen,

then opens his mouth to speak,
but I say,

> Let me go first.

He nods.

> I should be the one
> who doesn't trust you.
> I've told you everything,
> but you barely wanted to let me in.
>
> I get it. And I can't blame you for it.
> But if we're gonna try, really try,
> you have to trust me.

He leans against the white stove,
hugging himself.

> I know, JJ. I'm sorry.
> I doubt myself—and my judgment—so much now.
> I trusted my ex and she did something unforgivable.

> I understand. But I'm not her.

> I know, and I'm sorry I've been treating you
> like you are. It's just hard to get over.

> You know you didn't deserve what she did, right?

Trey looks like he's never thought of that before.
He chews on his lip, examines the kitchen.

I follow his eyes past the white refrigerator,
the short wooden dining table for two,
the toast-shaped clock on the wall.

> *Trey. It wasn't your fault.*

I hear what I'm telling him
and think of my dad.

Maybe deep down,
I thought *I* was the issue.

That if I had been a little more comforting
or if I was less of a reminder of my mama
or if I wasn't as heartbroken as both of them
that my dad wouldn't have vanished.

Trey places his face in his hands, rests
there for a moment before meeting my eyes.

> *That's the first time anyone has told me that.*
> *My parents told me all the ways*
> *I could have avoided that situation.*
> *They barely blamed her.*

I can only imagine what Trey went through.
My parents have always believed what I've told them.

> *You might have to forgive them before they forgive you,*
> I say.

Because I've learned that forgiveness
is for yourself,
not for anyone else.

Can I have a hug?
he asks, unfolding his arms.

I skate across the kitchen,
bury my face in his chest.
He wraps his arms around my waist
and rests his head on top of mine.

After a few minutes, I look up at him.

    You know I need to see these model cars, right?

He lets out a chuckle.

I already know.

He squeezes me tighter
and I return to my position on his chest.

I don't want to be anywhere else but here.

Who invited you, anyway?

    I ask as Trey and I go back downstairs.

Oh, my boy Mook. We've been chopping it up lately.

    Look at you, making new friends,
    I shout, the music overpowering my voice.

Trey joins Mook.
I join Tiana.

She starts a short and simple eight count.

Before I hop in,
I take my phone out
and text my dad.
Hey, let's meet soon.

My dad isn't perfect. No one is.
And if I'm telling Trey
to let go, to forgive,
I should do the same.
Or at least try.

I hop into Tiana's routine,
learn as I go.

    I think I want to host something like this,
    I say to Tiana.

A skate session?

> *Yeah, but on a bigger scale.*
> *In remembrance of WestSide Roll.*

Tiana bobs her head to the beat
and I take it as a nod.

It's a good idea.
People will definitely come out
if there's meaning behind it.
You gonna ask Mr. Mike?

> *Yeah. I think he'd love it.*

But where? The court I told you about is small,
Tiana says as she pivots to backward skate. I follow.

> *That court can't handle what I'm imagining.*
> *I think we should go where it all started,*
> *the WestSide Roll parking lot.*
> *It's huge, it's a place we love,*
> *and most skaters already have outdoor wheels.*

Okay, now I'm seeing the vision,
she says.

We skate around the basement
a few more times, arms linked,
repeating the routine,

making space
for each other

to soak up all the love in the room.

On my way home, I message Mr. Mike
on Facebook, the only social media he has.

I want his blessing,
don't want to honor something
he owned / loved / grew
without him.

Hey Mr. Mike. I hope you've been okay since WestSide Roll closed. I want to throw a remembrance party. I've been skating at a nearby tennis court and I think skaters could meet up in the WestSide Roll parking lot. I'm picturing snacks, a fire playlist, and everyone coming out to feel what WestSide Roll made us feel.

I miss it. Everyone else does. What do you think?

I press send,
body jittery,
excited for him to say yes.

Seventeen

TWENTY-FIVE DAYS SINCE WESTSIDE ROLL CLOSED

I scour my closet,
throwing options on the bed

and placing them back on the hanger
when a new idea strikes.

I've never even seen Trey's parents,
don't know if his mama wears

a bun, or a brooch on her shirt,
or if his dad is the clean-cut type

who doesn't grow a beard or have hobbies
outside of his corporate career.

My stomach houses an anchor
as I consider the options.

He hasn't had anything good
to say about either of them.

And I'm meeting them today
so I can see the model cars

that I now regret asking about.
I thought maybe Trey would bring them to me.

When he knocks on the front door,
the anchor drops further.

This is the fastest I've ever seen

Trey drive, one hand dangling out the window, other on the steering wheel.

Fingers tap. Tap. Tap.

What should I know about them?
I ask.

He acts like he doesn't hear me,
and I almost repeat myself until he says,

I don't even know where to start.

Finally, his list goes like this:

Stiff.

Joke sometimes.

The type of parents who ask "why are they buying Jordans instead of saving" about other people.

Used to be cool when I was younger.

Caring.

Very, very protective.

The drive isn't long,
would take ten minutes
if he wasn't speeding.

When we pull into his neighborhood,
almost every house is identical
two-story homes
with the same
paneling
roof
window treatment.

But a few cubic houses,
stark black or white, dot the neighborhood,
standing out like tulips
in a dandelion field.

He slows down drastically,
cruising through the neighborhood
like he's sightseeing.

There aren't too many kids playing
and if there are,
most of them don't look like us.

We walk up the driveway
to his front door.

The lawn-mower-striped grass
is so green it could stain jeans.

It reminds me of my old place.

Welcome to my humble abode,
he says, leads me in.

He instructs me to take my shoes off.

We go down the hallway,
pass the kitchen,
dining room,
living room,
grayscale family photos
decorating the walls

It feels untouched, unlived-in.
So tidy it's almost medical.

> *Aww, look at you!*
> I stop and gush about a baby photo of him.

Baby Trey cheeses with no teeth,
looks up at the camera,
arms wide, fingers spread like he's about to clap.

Same cute face now as I had then,
he says, beaming at the photo.

    I roll my eyes.
    Here you go.

Trey takes a deep breath
as we stand in front of their glass patio door.

    Should I be scared?
    I whisper.

My feet sink into the plush cream carpet,
my toes grip the fibers to ground me.
I take another look around.
Everything is cream and black, nothing out of place.

    Are we going out there?
    I don't have any shoes on.

We're gonna say hi
from the door.

He grips the handle
then slides the door open and says,
Mom. Dad.
Jaelyn is here.

I smile and wave through the slit.

They size me up,
looking from my bare feet

to my natural hair
that's down at my shoulders today.

Hello, Jaelyn.
Nice to meet you,
his mom says,
the pink in her sundress
making her light skin sparkle.

I study her face and don't see Trey in it
but his dad,
who echoes a *hello,*
is an older Trey.

Same skin tone,
body build,
similar voice.

> *It's so nice to meet you both.*
> I smile, all teeth.

We're gonna go to my room,
Trey says.

His parents get up from their outdoor sectional,
his mom with an empty wineglass in hand.

I know you didn't think
we'd let her in your room
without us being inside, his mom says.

Never thought that at all.

He looks down at the carpet.

We move out of the way
for them to come in.

His dad says,
Door open. You two have an hour.

My mama has the same rule
but her tone never sounds like theirs.

She gives me some freedom,
they seem to want to take his away.

Trey's room is neater than I imagined.

I expected chaos.

A pile of clothes thrown in a corner,
games strewn across the room.

But everything has a place.
His king-size bed is made,
his PS5 on the TV stand looks untouched.

So where are these cars?
Was this just a trick to get me in your room?
I ask, spinning around, looking for them.

Shhh, why are you yelling?

Is it a secret? I thought they knew.

He shrugs.
They did. They don't know I'm still making them.

He approaches the closet,
I stay near his bedroom door.

You can sit on the bed.

He rummages through the walk-in closet,
tossing things over his shoulder
like a cartoon character.

Finally, a hush falls over the room.

Come here, he says.

I go to the closet. Each pair of pants is on an S-hook,
each pair of basketball shorts is folded on the top shelf.

Trey kneels at the bottom and looks up at me,
a shiny red model car in his palm like a platter.

This is a Porsche 911 Carrera 4S.
2019. Worth about $200.

I crouch next to him
and study the collection,
every color you can think of
in a glass display case.

> *These are beautiful.*
> *How much time do they take?*

Forever.

> *How'd you start?*

Trey explains that when he and his dad
used to go to car shows, he'd write down all the cars he loved,
knew that even though his parents made good money

it might never be enough to afford luxury cars.
So to have them all, this was his solution.

I listen as he educates me on every car in the case,
why he loves it, what inspired the color,
the tools he used to build it.

I'm completely captivated.
He talks about building model cars
like he aches to make them.

> *Why did you think this was stupid?*
> *It's so cool.*

He places a yellow truck back in the display case.
Telling a girl you make model cars
doesn't exactly get you the girl.

My friends clowned me.
My parents thought it was a waste of time.
So I've learned to keep it to myself.

I walk my hand to his.

> *If it's worth anything,*
> *your love for this makes me like you even more.*

Trey uses his other hand to rub the back of his neck,
he makes eye contact,
then his gaze falls to my lips.

JJ, if we weren't here, I'd kiss you.

Eighteen

THIRTEEN DAYS UNTIL THE WESTSIDE ROLL REMEMBRANCE PARTY

Trey cruises down 38th Street,
one arm behind my headrest.

This party is a dope idea,
he says.

Ever since I messaged Mr. Mike,
I've blown up Noe, Trey, and my mama

with ideas about decor,
music,
who to invite.

> *Thank you,*
> I respond.
> *You ready to show off your skills?*

To the whole skate community?
Nah, y'all got it.

> Come on, Trey.
> You've gotten so good.

Mm, we'll see.

For me?

I ask, puppy eyes activated.

I study his face.

I can never get over
his butter-smooth brown skin,

his sharp jawline,
his dancing eyes
and adorable lips.

That's not fair.
You know it's anything for you.
His smile gleams.

The sun peeks through his tints.

Are you going to invite your dad?

I don't know about all that.
I haven't even thought that far.

I feel it.

Trey turns the music back up,
Ari Lennox crooning
as we pull into WestSide Roll's lot.

Noe should be here soon,
I say as we wait.

Trey turns to me and kisses
me on the forehead.

Before Noelle gets here,
I want to say that you have made my move
here so much easier, Trey says.
I was so alone at first, so ready to beg my parents
to move back even though I hated it there.
But when I met you, that changed.

> *You've made this summer less lonely for me, too.*
> *You've made it worth remembering.*

I lean in to kiss him,
the center console separating
our bodies, but we only move closer.

Oh, knock it off!
Noe says as she approaches Trey's car.
When we get out, she gives us a once-over.

Get a room next time.

> *Girl, hush,* I say, laughing.

She opens her Notes app
and we look around at the empty lot.
Even though a brewery is replacing WestSide Roll,
there aren't any cars, construction, signs.

I'm here, at your service,
Noe says.

I told her Trey and I could handle planning,
but she said she'd feel worse if she stayed at home worrying.

> I point to the sidewalk in front of the building.
> *That's where the food table can go.*
> *It's giving . . . chips, pops, and waters.*

Trey asks, *We can't serve nachos?*

> *So we can clean up cheese all night? No.*
> I veto it before he can get any other ideas.

Sometimes Trey just says anything.

>   *I want it to give WestSide Roll vibes*
>   *as much as possible.*

Okay, so disco balls?
Maybe tiny ones that can hang
from the building?
Trey asks.

I'm not America's Next Top Designer,
but disco balls hanging from a brick building is an interesting choice.

>   *Mmm, I don't know about that either.*
>   *Doesn't even sound possible.*

What? I think it'll be nice!

>   *That's the issue*, I say, and laugh.
>   Noe joins in, shaking her head,
>   probably imagining the same nightmare I am.

>   *What about a Bluetooth disco ball speaker or two?*

Noe jots it down and pulls up a picture,
bright lights shining through the silver
in the product photo.

Okay, that's a better idea than mine.
You got me, Trey says.

>   I keep going, directing.

And then we can do metallic fringe streamers on the building, instead.

I've never considered myself a planner.
But this is an extension of the place
I can't believe I'm living without.

And that feels like second nature to me.

Let's skate before we hit the road,
I say once logistics are done.

We run to the cars for our skates—
Noe is driving Nate's today.

I'm gonna record our session if that's okay,
Trey says.

Neither of us protest.
He pulls a phone tripod out of his backpack.

*You trying to steal the camera job from
WestSide Roll's one-and-only Ron?* I ask, laughing.

Never. Trying to be his understudy,
he jokes.

Beyoncé booms through the speaker.

I slip my skates on so fast
I almost lose balance.
I tie them quickly,
loop around the ankles,
make a bow in the front.

I start skating,
imagine maneuvering
through a thick crowd.

Noe grabs onto me
and Trey grabs onto her.
They move their feet the same way I do,
spin and cross their feet in sync with mine.

We skate like the rink has been gone for years.

Sweat trickles down my neck to my back,
makes a path for more droplets to travel.

The steamy heat grasps my body as we go around.
The sunset pinks the sky.

My feet ache
from the quickness
of our movements.

My arms are in the sky,
reaching,
reaching

for that feeling,
for that freedom.

Once we stop to take a breath, Noe asks,
Where is the water?

    I forgot!

You're trying to dehydrate
the planning committee.
She huffs, wipes her forehead
with the back of her hand.

    The party will have plenty
    of water. I promise.

I hope so, 'cause you need to be sued,
Trey jumps in.

They laugh together.
I watch them bend, cover their mouths,
and crack up on my behalf.

I drink up their laughter.
Let it fill me, warm me,
give me hope.

Babe, you wanna skate by yourself?
For the video?

    Um, sure. Babe.

I start the playlist again and it spits out R&B.

I move with a softness,

close my eyes, hug myself,

and sway

to a melody that

                    swells

takes up

        all the space

in the lot.

We crowd around Trey's phone to watch.

He whistles and says,
Ayeee, you look nice.
Can I post this?
His eyes are stuck on the video,
as mesmerized as me.

> *That should be the party invitation,*
> I say.

So you *should post it.*

Trey sends me the video
before I find an excuse.

When I watch it from my phone,
I look like someone else.

Maybe my mama.
Maybe my dad.
Maybe Tiana.
Maybe Mr. Kareem.
Maybe Mook and Lailani.
Maybe Miss Charlene.
Maybe Mr. Mike.

I see each of my influences
in the way I let my body take charge.

My motions are bigger

and they don't struggle to be seen anymore,

for they're the only thing

in the video

worth looking at.

The caption:

A few weeks ago, I lost one of the most important places to me: WestSide Roll. It held so many of my memories. It's where I met some of the people closest to me.

I miss it. I miss having a guaranteed Saturday night plan at a place that won't kick me and my friends out for being loud and Black. I miss knowing that I'm gonna see the same people every weekend.

This is a long way to say, I decided to do something about it. Almost two weeks from today, I want everyone to meet me at the WestSide Roll parking lot in Indy, 6 p.m. Bring your skates and outdoor wheels, bring your friends, bring your love. Leave the drama.

As we gather our skates to leave
a patrol car enters the lot.

The cop pulls his car behind our parked ones
and rolls down his window.

What are you all doing here?
He doesn't bother removing his sunglasses.

Just skating,
Noelle says, turning to look at him.
Trey and I turn with her.

I gulp
loudly enough
for everyone to hear.

You can't skate here.

    Where does it say that?
    I ask.

It's private property,
he says.

Trey mumbles,
Let's go before he starts asking for IDs.
I can't get in any more trouble.

Noe cuts her eyes at him
ready to challenge the officer.

Yeah, let's go.

Noe, get in with us for a minute,

I say in a hushed voice.

We turn away from the officer
and get in.
Once I'm seated,
Trey starts the car.

I lean against the headrest,
close my eyes.

The pit of my stomach stirs.

That could have gone so many ways,
I say.

Trey and Noe don't respond.

I'm deep under my covers
watching *Abbott Elementary*
when my phone rings with a FaceTime.

>   *Ughhh*, I groan.

But I realize it's Trey
and I'm no longer bothered.

>   *Are you feeling okay?*
>   *After what happened earlier?*
>   I ask when I answer.

My bonnet is damn near
to my eyebrows, eyes tired.
The blue light from my screen illuminates my face.

Yeah, I've been through worse,
he responds.

We both gaze at each other,
lost in thought.

I think you're going viral,
he says, breaking the trance.

>   *What?*

I sit up, turn the bedside lamp on.
I turned off my social notifications
because it's been a long day,

week,

few weeks.

The video is at 4K views already.

> *How?* I ask. *I don't even post.*
> *I only posted this so I could DM it to people*
> *to invite them.*

It's your good looks.

> *Trey, stop it,*
> I say, laughing and rolling my eyes.

But for real, a skater we follow
reposted it and it's blowing up.
Everyone's saying they love your energy.

I navigate to my profile so fast I don't remember getting there.

> *It's at 4.5K views now,*
> I say low and slow,
> surprised.

I don't know if you wanted
the party to be this big,
but it's gonna be huge.

I scroll through the comments,
shocked at all the skaters who say
they'll drive up

or drive down

or tell their friends.

A loss for one skater is a loss for all,

one of the comments says.

I read each one,

searching

for Mr. Mike.

Nineteen

TWELVE DAYS UNTIL THE WESTSIDE ROLL REMEMBRANCE PARTY

My rules for today:

    1. If my dad is late, don't go with him.

    2. Say how I feel, no matter what.

    3. Consider forgiving him.

He took a half day from work
to spend time with me.

I was thinking a few hours max.

I stand near the front door, waiting
like I did all those times when he never showed.
I pick at the chipped wall,
watch the light gray paint fall to the ground.

He knocks two minutes
before the time he said he'd arrive.

Progress.

I open the door too quickly,
he tilts his head in confusion.

Hey, baby girl.
More of a question.

> *I was in the kitchen*
> *getting some water,*
> I lie, no glass in my hand,
> mouth dry as crackers.

Uh, okay. You ready?
We're going somewhere new.

> *Yep.*

I walk out of the door behind him,
heart beating like an 808.

We park at the cupcake shop.

The awning is bright pink,
the cursive storefront sign
white with sprinkles.

"You're the frosting
to my cupcake"
is painted on the glass in yellow.

I thought we could use a switch-up from ice cream,
plus I can't handle lactose like I used to.
My dad rubs his stomach.

I study the shop through the windshield,
watch white women in multicolor athleisure
go in and out, some ushering their kids along.

> *Have you tried it?*
> I ask.

Nope. I've been waiting
to try them with you.
I heard they're the best in town.

> *We'll see about that,*
> I say as I swing open the passenger door.

It's even brighter inside.
The walls are hot pink, the display cases don
baby pink name cards. The menu, three mounted screens
side by side, is also pink.

They have every kind of cake you can think of,
from mini cupcakes to jumbo,
from cheesecake to lemon.
My eyes jump from one screen to the other.

Wanna share a jumbo?
Like we used to share sundaes?

He's trying so hard that I don't know
if I'm appreciative or annoyed.

Sure.

The cupcake is as big

as me and my dad's heads put together.

He sits on one side of the pink booth,
I slide into the seat across from him.

His face is so different now,
lacks the joy he used to have.

I remember when skaters would latch onto
my dad like Velcro the minute he walked into a room.

They wanted to soak up his sun.
They wanted to revel in his energy.

Now he's more reserved,
his voice doesn't boom with the same bass.

He's lost much more than I thought.

My dad's fork hovers
over the red velvet cupcake,

white icing topping it
like a vanilla soft serve cone.

Ready to dig in?
he asks.

I grab my fork
and we go for it.

I plop a huge piece into my mouth
and it's perfectly sweet,

doesn't leave me wanting more,
doesn't make me want less.

I can't believe I've been missing out on this.

We tear the cupcake up
like it's our last meal,

leaving nothing but crumbs
in the disposable cake cup.

    Whew, I say,
        lean back and let my food baby protrude.

He does the same,
spreads out on his side of the table.

I know I haven't been around
like I should have been, he says.

He's right.

He could have visited

could have called on my birthday

could have stuck to the plans he suggested.

If someone wants to do something,
they're gonna find a way.

They'll move mountains
and stars   and skies if they have to.

And he didn't move a thing.

I'm sorry,
he says.

Finally. The only words I've wanted to hear
for so long.

He's given me everything *but* an apology,
and at this point, I don't know if it's enough.

I dig deep down for the courage
to fight for myself.

I've been able to do it
at work
with Noe
with Trey

but each time,
the relationship falls apart.

This time, though, there's nothing to break.
Me and my dad are already broken.

> *Why now? Why not when I thought about*
> *you every day and wondered when you'd visit?*

> *It feels like you're apologizing*
> *because I'm learning to be okay without you.*

> *I don't deserve that.*

I've never stood up to my dad or told him
how he's made me feel 'cause you don't
tell your parents about themselves.

They tell you.

I keep going,
not letting him interrupt
to apologize again.

I tell him how
WestSide Roll was my connection
to him and Mama.

I tell him it wasn't
fair to lose him,
then find myself
in the rink only
to kinda lose him again.

It's not fair that
he waited for the loss
of something we both loved
to come back to me.

It takes everything in me
not to run away
take cover
after laying my feelings flat.

Now it's his turn
to find some courage.

I look between us,

thinking of all the things

I inherited from him:

His nose.

His rhythm.

His loud laugh.

His cowardice.

You're right.

*I didn't know how to see you
without remembering how much
you and your mama and our life meant to me.*

*I should have told you.
You're old enough to understand that.
But I didn't want you to hate me.*

> *Well, disappearing wasn't the best method.*

My dad uses his fork
to play with the cake crumbs.

I play with mine.

For a few minutes,
only the sounds of squeaking shoes
and the cashier's voice
fill the space.

> *I forgive you,*
> I say.

Because I'm ready to do it for me.
I'm ready to tear down the walls
he's caused me to put up.

> *You can apologize a million times
> but I need more than that.*

> *I deserve consistency and communication*
> *and all the things I get from the people who show me*
> *they love me.*

> *If you're not willing to show up for me,*
> *I can't show up just for you to*
> *disappoint me again.*

For the first time in years,
he's given me the space
to speak instead of bombarding me
with his guilt.

I understand,
he finally says, and stands up,
towering over me.

Jaelyn, I will always love you.
It would be a privilege for us to get back to a good place.
I'm going to work hard to make sure we do.

> *I hope so,*
> I say, still seated.

He holds his arms out for a hug.
I'm reluctant.

You gonna leave me hanging?
he asks, face falling.

I should,
I say.

He starts to lower his arms
but I get up,

walk into his hug,
and remember how,
when I wanted to feel safe,
he would let me hide right here.

As my dad drives me home,

Mr. Mike's name appears on my screen.
I click on it, enter my passcode,
will the phone to load faster.

His gray paragraph is

long

long

long

as a bus route.

My dad talks, but I don't hear a word.
I read the message fully.
Mr. Mike cites all the reasons
he shouldn't go:
- Too soon
- Too painful
- Too much for him to handle
- Too much of a reminder of what he couldn't keep

I thought Mr. Mike would need this
as much as I do.

I should have considered that he'd be too hurt
to see the good in us all skating together again.

But what is a party for WestSide Roll
if he's not there to celebrate?

Jaelyn, did you hear me?

My dad interrupts my train of thought.

    Huh?

I said I love you,
he says, backing into a spot
in my complex.

    Oh.

No need to say it back.
I just need you to know.

I text Trey before I get out the car.

Mr. Mike said no
and I just got back from dessert
with my dad ☹

He replies.

Don't worry. I got something for you.

Thanks for hanging with me today.
Maybe we can do this weekly?
my dad asks.

    I turn to him with bulged eyes,
    gripping the door handle.
    Every week?

Okay, every two.

    That I can do.

    Thanks for showing up.

I don't know if I should
applaud a fish for swimming
but even if I never say it to his face,

I missed him
so,
so
much.

By the time I walk through the front door, Trey has sent me an invitation he made on Canva, complete with animated burgers, that reads

A SLIDER-EATING COMPETITION
Where: Assortments
When: Tonight, 6 p.m.
Who's Paying: Me, of course
Why: Because we have a lot to chew on

I laugh, unable to rein my smile in.

Me: You have way too much time on your hands 🤭

Trey: Always enough time for you 😘

Assortments's patio seating is mostly empty,
save a family that probably lives across the street.
This area—Meridian Kessler—is the 'burbs, just walkable.

The host takes us to our table and Trey pulls out my chair.
Once I'm seated, he leans down and whispers,

Prepare to lose.

As I flip from the front to the back
of the menu, Trey rubs his hands
together like he's warming them.

*I don't know why you think
you're gonna win*, I say.

Trey only smiles.

Yeah, okay, he says.
What are you ordering?

Assortments is a sampler restaurant.
They have everything—all types of fries,
sauces, sandwiches, sliders, shakes.
Fancier than Steak 'n Shake for sure.

I pass him my filled-out menu,
with avocado, zucchini, and sweet potato fries,
steak and chicken burgers, spicy sauces,
and sweet shakes checked off.

Trey frowns.

Ewww, he says. *Avocado fries?*
I know we're in a bougie area, but come on.

    Ain't nothing wrong with my fry choices,
        I say, giggling at his scrunched-up expression.
    What are you *getting?*

He passes his menu over.

*Classic. I'm tryna see if their chicken sandwich
is better than Popeyes's.*

    There's nothing classic about this, I say,
    looking at his white truffle ketchup
    and other odd sauce choices.

He rubs his hands together
again, smirking over his fingertips.

Trey tucks his napkin in the neckline
of his shirt like a bib.
I place mine on my lap.

>*You are so goofy*, I say.

You love it, he says back,
smiles up at me then at his spread.
Before we start, do you wanna talk about today?

>*Honestly? No. What are the rules?* I ask,
>trying to strategize instead.

*First one to finish every part
of the assortment, shake shots
included, wins. But you can alter the opponent's
table arrangement however you like.*

He smirks. I smirk back.

>*Well, start the timer, Trey,
>so we can remember how quickly I beat you.*

I chow down on my sides first,
planning to go to milkshakes next.

But as I chew, Trey reaches
his long arm over the table,
scrambles my food.

>*Stop*, I shout, mouth full.

I try to reach his, but he shields
everything with one arm, picks up
his food with the other.

> *Cheater!* I say, and laugh, arranging
> my food with my left, grabbing shakes
> and mixing them into one cup with my right.

That's not fair, he says, looking at all
the food he has left.

We keep eating, grinning at each other
like it's part of the game.

We're both almost done,
too focused on winning to
scramble food again.

Final countdown, Trey says,
mouth full of fries, ends jutting out.

I focus on his lips for too long,
enough time for him to be one
or two mouthfuls—depending on
how he plays it—away from winning.

I get up and sit on his lap, blocking his way.

JJ, that's cheating.
He laughs, still finishing his fries.
Before he can think about lifting me
off him, I wrap my calves around his, lock them,
make separation impossible.

But my legs don't matter.
Trey turns sideways, my body
now facing away from the table.

He picks up his last bite,
chews quickly, swallows.
Throws his hands up in victory.

It doesn't pay to mind
someone else's business,
does it? he asks.

Hush, I say.

He wraps his arms around my waist,
rests his cheek on my back.

His fingers trail up and down my arm,
the feel of his fingertips making the butterflies
in my stomach dance.

*I've been wanting to ask you something
but I know it's been a hard few weeks,*
he says to my back.

I'll answer any question that will take my mind off it.

*We've kinda talked
about this before, but I was wondering—*

He stops,
taps the side of my thigh.

I want to face you,
he says, and stands once I do.

Every part of my body prickles
with nerves.

*I don't want to be with anyone else
but you. I know I've said it's hard to trust,
but you've made me rethink what love is.
In a good way.*

*And I know you have a hard time accepting love
but, Jaelyn, I'm here. I don't plan on going anywhere.*

Maybe I should have started this more positively . . .
He trails off, stuffs his hands in his pockets.

Will you be my girlfriend?

*I think if we forgive everybody
who made us feel the way we did
about love, we'll be unstoppable.*

I'm speechless,
eyes locked on his.

What if we could be?

When I'm with Trey

I'm invincible,

I can take on anything.

It's okay to say no, JJ.
Trey looks down, disappointed.
I step closer to him and closer
until our faces are centimeters apart.

> *Trey, there's no boyfriend
> I'd rather have.
> Yes.*

I grab his chin,

bring his lips to mine,

and we kiss so deep

his hands find me and rest on the small of my back.

This is my boyfriend

from head to toe.

He is the *what if*

I'm willing to take a chance on.

Twenty

SIX DAYS UNTIL THE WESTSIDE ROLL REMEMBRANCE PARTY

I reach WestSide Roll
and my body still gets excited
like I'll be able to go in
and skate again.
But when I get close to the entrance
there's a new sign
bolted into the grass beside it.
It's white with red letters yelling

NO TRESPASSING

VIOLATORS WILL BE PROSECUTED

What makes me a trespasser
in my own neighborhood?

What makes me a trespasser
when I spent every weekend here,
loved it,
supported it?

Rage roils in me,
heats my insides.

This sign changes everything.

The party is in six days.

The tennis courts at the Indy Parks are booked

and no place else is big or cheap enough to host us.

While I stand at the bus stop,

I FaceTime Noe and Trey on the same call.
I don't want to explain this more than once.

They finally answer.

> *I can't have the skate party anymore,*
> I say.

Oh, stop being dramatic,
Noe says.
And why do you have me
on the phone with Trey?

Trey says,
I'm wondering the same thing.
His voice raspy, like he just woke up.

> *Y'all, I'm serious.*
> *There's a no trespassing sign up now.*

Before they can ask more questions,
I send the proof.
They stare at the photo
as long as I did the real thing.

You lying,
Trey says.

> *I wish I was. I don't understand.*
> *We were literally just there.*

That's probably why.
That patrol cop or whatever
wanted us gone. Forever,
Noe says as she moves around her apartment.

I don't even know what to say.
Trey shakes his head.

> *I don't either.*
> *What am I gonna do?*

You could tell Mr. Mike.
Noe is always quick on her feet
with an answer.

> *I don't know about all that.*
> *He already said he doesn't want to come.*

It's worth a try,
Trey chimes in.

I should have just let WestSide Roll
go
like Noe said weeks ago.

On the bus ride home

I waffle between

maybe it's not meant to be
and
maybe this is what gentrification
looks like
and
maybe it is too soon
and
maybe
maybe
maybe

Draft one to Mr. Mike in my Notes app:

Hey, Mr. Mike. I know you said you don't want to come to the skate party. But I need your advice. Can you call me?

Never sent.

Draft two to Mr. Mike in my Notes app:

Hey, Mr. Mike. There's a no trespassing sign up at WestSide Roll now and I can't throw the party. Do you have any advice? So many skaters from different cities said they're coming and I don't want to let the skate community down. I understand if you don't want to be involved.

Never sent.

Draft three to Mr. Mike in my Notes app:

Hey, Mr. Mike. I hope you're doing okay. I didn't want to be the one who brought this to you, but there's a no trespassing sign in front of WestSide Roll now, where the remembrance party is happening. What should I do?

Never sent.

FOUR DAYS UNTIL THE WESTSIDE ROLL REMEMBRANCE PARTY

I finally get the courage
to bother Mr. Mike again,
for real this time,

because we deserve more
than being called unlawful
in our own neighborhood.

Draft four in my Notes app:

*Hey, Mr. Mike. I know you don't want to come out
to the party, but do you have any advice on what to do
about this?*
*So many skaters want to honor WestSide Roll, I don't want
to let them down.*

I attach the photo.

He reads it
and I watch the "typing" bubble
for what feels like months.

I'm on it, Jaelyn, he says.
Don't even worry about it.

But I do worry.
As I find something to stream.

As I check my messages repeatedly
for more details from Mr. Mike.
As more and more skaters comment
on the original post and say they can't wait to road-trip.

THREE DAYS UNTIL THE WESTSIDE ROLL REMEMBRANCE PARTY

I walk into the cupcake shop,
scan the pink-drenched booths
for Mr. Mike.

Meeting here was his suggestion.
I guess it's not half bad.

I find his bald head within a few seconds and stroll over,
then hover beside his table.

I didn't know which one you'd like,
Mr. Mike says, gesturing at both cupcake flavors.

I slide into the seat opposite him,
thank him, and grab the birthday cake cupcake.

*So what do I need to do
to make this party happen?*
I sink my fork into the plushness.

Nothing. I handled it.

*What? Mr. Mike, I only needed your advice.
I didn't want you to put any work in.*

*I'm never gonna leave y'all hanging.
No matter what,* he says. *WestSide Roll
was never about me. It's always been about community.*

> *I can't thank you enough,*
> I say.

He dives into the details.
Even though the tennis courts were booked up,
he pulled some strings with his friend at Indy Parks.

They were college roommates
who go way way back.
As all oldheads say,
He owed me a favor.

> *So where is the party now?*
> I ask.

Riverside Park Tennis Court Complex.

Unlike the raggedy tennis court
that's walking distance from me,
Riverside Park has three courts joined together.

Indy Parks has kept them sparkling
because the new amphitheater
at Riverside brings increased traffic—and donations.

It's smooth enough to not damage our wheels.

It's large enough for all the skaters coming.

It's exactly what I'd hoped for.

Twenty-One

Today is the day.

We pull up to Riverside's
empty tennis courts—
me, Noe, and Trey in one car,
Tiana trailing us in another.

My mama stayed home with Granny.

The smell of chicken grilling
makes its way into Trey's car,
music intertwines so we hear
different beats, lyrics that belong elsewhere.

Riverside Park is always like this in the summer.
People grill and throw birthday parties
under the many for-rent gazebos

full of Black people ready to eat,
ready to dance,
ready to come together.

Children overrun the actual park area,
swarming the slides and swings and monkey bars.

The tennis courts are spotless,
a clean that can only be achieved by constant care.

We pile out of the cars,
pop the trunks, but when I reach
for the cooler in Trey's, he stops me.

*Please go relax. You did all
the planning, we got everything else,* he says.

But I need to do something or I'll panic.

He puts down the case of Sprite he was holding.

Bring it in, he says.

I get in his space
and he bear-hugs me,
rocking me back and forth.

*Tonight is going to be great.
You dreamed this up and we're all
here to make it happen. Okay?*

I sigh.
Okay.

It's been thirty minutes and no one is here.

All of the decor is up,
including a cheap photo backdrop
and skate-related props to take pictures with.

I skate back and forth on the court
to silence, won't start
our playlist until we need to.

People are going to show,
Noe says. Trey and Tiana
nod in agreement.

But if they don't, if they accidentally
go to the original location,
or if they find something better to do,
then I've lost it all twice.

I catch Noe's glance to Trey,
who shoots a quick glance at Tiana.

> *What's wrong?*
> I ask.

I don't need anyone hiding anything
from me today.

Nothing, girl,
Noe pipes up.
We just want you to be patient.

Everyone nods in agreement,
and Noe assures me again.
People will show.
Why wouldn't they?

Because people have better things to do
than skate at some tennis courts, I say.

I don't know any skater
with something better to do on a weekend,
Noe says, and cracks a smile.

Girl, the shade,
I say, laughing with her.

Tiana joins in the laughter.
I think they'll be close one day.
I imagine us all hanging out at whatever place
will embrace us.
Having sleepovers.
Sharing gossip.

Before everyone gets here,
we got something for you,
Noe says.

Tiana pulls a black shirt
out of her crossbody bag, unrolls it.

It reads "Long Live WestSide Roll" on the front
in the same thick purple script as the rink's logo,
then she flips it and my social handles are on the back.

Even though you're not in a crew,
we thought you should have this,
Trey says.

I can barely contain my happiness.
I grab the shirt, rub the soft cotton,
throw it on over my cropped black tank.
I hug them, strong and tight.

    Thanks, y'all. It's perfect.

Then there's bass roaring from cars, shaking the court's gates.
Then parking spots get taken one by one, flashy cars
   beside each other, tints dark as blacktop.
Then everyone pours out, droves of skaters,
   holding skates by their sides or by their knotted laces,
   or skating toward us. All of them in black like we asked.
   'Cause we're mourning.

It's a reunion at first,

everyone shaking up and hugging,
telling each other how good they look.

It's only been a few weeks,
but we're used to often.

> Start the playlist please

I text the group chat.

The music booms.
The perfect first song,
the same one DJ Sunny kicked off Saturdays with.

The people who only dance
designate themselves to a corner,
rap the lyrics.

Some lean against the gate
like it's the short purple wall
at WestSide Roll,
others walk around and mingle.

We know how to do this.
We know how to make a place home.

Six p.m. was the perfect start time.

It's not burning up   not cold from a night draft.
It's not so early that it interrupts Saturday errands
                but not so late that no one showed.

Great for everyone to groove.

The courts are so crowded now that I can't find
Noe, Tiana, or Trey. Our speakers are so loud
that people have to shout over the music.

Some people scream in laughter
as someone tells them a joke.

Some skaters throw their hands high
like their fingertips could brush the clouds.

Some parents hold their child's hand
as they skate slowly through the court.

Some people are visiting from other cities,
accents dripping from their tongues.

Trey wraps his arms around me
and skates behind me, our feet in sync.

We bop and glide, knees bending with the beat,
arms up to make ourselves bigger
or arms in to tuck ourselves into a trick.

Naptown Rollers,
NapSk8z,
WestSide Riders fly past, routines
        fluid like they were born
           performing them.

We ebb and flow
into each other,
whistles blow.

As one song transitions into another,
we erupt, squeezing through
any empty space.

My dad rolls up to me.
I never saw him arrive.

I'm proud of you, baby girl.
This is amazing,
he says.

Even his sweat towel is black today.
He holds it in his hand
like a comfort item.

> *Thank you,*
> I say.
> *Who'd you come with?*

He points as he explains,
Bobby over there, and a few other folks
who used to be in my skate crew.

> *Don't break a knee,*
> I say, and laugh.

We're being careful
so we don't have to sue you.

> *Thanks for bringing all of those people out.*

They saw your video and told me *about it.*

They got the scoop on me about my own baby girl.

Could you let me know next time?

he asks.

I look out at the mass of black,
feeling full.

    Yeah, I can do that.

The sun starts to set

and that's when we really flow.

Tiana and Miss Charlene

and Mr. Kareem and Mook

and Lailani

find us and join.

Ron trails behind, recording.

We're one,

a Black herd.

We swing in

and out of clusters,

toe spin, footwork

through the courts.

They can snatch our neighborhood,

steal our livelihood,

but they can never

take us away from

each other.

Heyyy, Mr. Mike,
I hear someone shout.

I spin to find Mr. Mike
entering the gate,
skates in hand,
ready to roll.

I glide to him,
beaming like a disco ball when light hits it.
He never said he'd change his mind.

> Mr. Mike, oh my God!
> Thank you for coming.
> I know you didn't plan on it.
> You helped more than enough.

Well, after that video, your dad reached out
and asked if he'd see me there.
Then the rest of your people
told me how much it meant to you.
Your mom.
And Noelle.
And Trey.
And Tiana.

Did you ask them to do that?
he asks.

I scan the court,

can't find their plotting asses anywhere.

Not at all.

Well, you have some people who care.

It means a lot for you to be here.

It means a lot
that WestSide Roll
meant so much to everybody.

The last set of slow songs
graces the speakers.
We saved the best
for those who stayed.

It's a little less packed
and there's more room to fill.

So I take advantage.

Trey and I find each other,
join hands once we hear the intro to our song,
"Make It Last Forever."

He leads the way,
his back facing everyone,
staring me in the eyes.

People part as we skate like they know we don't see anyone else.

It reminds me of our first time skating together:
my heart uncontrollable, his palms clammy,
only breaking focus to not run into others.

The magic with Trey—
the falling—never stops.

> *I'm so lucky to have you*, I say.
> And I'm scared that I am, but I am happy, too.

He smiles, dimples crescents on his cheeks.

I am, too, JJ. I love you.

    I love you, too.

For the first time on skates,
we kiss, still moving,
his feet still guiding me.

Skaters leave reluctantly,
opposite of how they arrived.

Noe tears tables down,
packing what's left.

Mr. Mike finds me again.

This felt . . . good. Right,
he says.

>   *It did,* I say.

Good job. Maybe it's your turn
to keep skating in Indy alive.

Before I can thank him again,
he walks off
and I watch
until he vanishes
into the parking lot.

We stand in the lot once we've packed the last of the trunks.
Skaters still mingle like it's WestSide Roll,
not planning to leave until someone says so.

Drivers do burnouts in the next lot over,
smoke from the tires rising as people cheer on the sidelines.

I almost forget that the rink isn't up the street anymore
because we fell into the same routine,
danced the same dance.

The energy of WestSide Roll lives on.

Trey, don't get into no accident.
You're riding with a real Naptown legend now.
I would hate to have to rough
you up for getting my best friend
in some trouble,
Noe says to Trey as we stand
near his car. It's me and him tonight.

Tiana nods, cosigning.

Yes, ma'am, Trey says.

We get in and Trey lets the windows down,
the gusts of night wind refreshing.

Where you wanna go? he asks.

    I'm fine just riding around with you,
I say.

He rests his right hand
on my thigh, gives it a squeeze
as we pull off.

I made us a playlist.

He presses play, places his phone
in the cupholder and the playlist name
displays on the car screen:
"Make it last forever."

We sing as Trey races down
the highway.

We ride until each song
has been sung, screamed,
wailed. Curfew be damned.

Acknowledgments

The thing about taking forever to write a novel is that you have loads of people to thank. I am grateful for every single person who has shaped my debut journey, some of whom will continue to shape the world around me and every book I write. Without y'all, this book wouldn't exist. *Under the Neon Lights* is an ode to community, so here's my ode to mine.

Always first, I want to thank God, who has listened to all my prayers and questions and guided me softly through each of them. Without you, there are so many leaps of faith I wouldn't have taken. I thank you for this path—every good step and misstep, every decision that has shone light on something new, every glimmer of hope you've shown me each time I've wanted to give up.

Thank you to my wonderful agent, Jodi Reamer. Our first conversation during my LitUp fellowship sealed the deal for me. I always knew you were the agent I wanted, and our conversation flowed like we were friends. Thank you for your fierce negotiation, your humor and pep talks, and your dedication to my career. We're such a power team!

To my wonderful editors, Tiara Kittrell and Rūta Rimas—thank you for seeing who Jaelyn is and *why* she is. For understanding what it means for young Black girls to find their voice and use it loudly. For understanding my vision with UTNL and doing everything you can to execute it. For forever being excited about the future skating party where we will all fall again and again!

Thank you to the rest of my awesome team at PRH: Lathea

Mondesir, Jaleesa Davis, Christina Colangelo, Bri Lockhart, Jessie Clark, Felicity Vallence, Summer Ogata, Natalie Vielkind, Alex Campbell, Theresa Evangelista, Betsy Cola, Jen Klonsky, Jen Loja, and everyone who worked on this book.

Thank you, Mama. Your love for education and writing made me the author and reader I am today. I cannot thank you enough for your endless support, advice, jokes, and cheering. You always ground me and remind me that what I'm writing matters. Thank you for investing in me in so many ways—from providing everything a parent should to showing up even when I'm far away. You are my number one fan, and I am yours.

Thank you to my dad. You showed me how to express myself through art. You had me on a stage when I was just a timid little girl. You taught me how to be confident. You are the reason I love music and writing, taking me to poetry events and showing me your own before I even knew how to appreciate it. Whenever I write, you say, "Keep going." I'll always appreciate your endless support.

Grandma: Thank you for raising me to follow my dreams. Every step of the way, you've told me that you believe in me and that you're proud. I'm so glad that you are here to see my first novel in the world. I can't wait to hear you brag on the phone to your friends about this even more.

To Auntie Dana and Cheyanne: Every day, you show me the importance of having an extended family who loves, cares for, and treats me like their own daughter/sister. Thank you for cheering me on.

To Leah Johnson: One of my best friends, my mentor, the other half of Duffy Gang—UTNL wouldn't have existed if it weren't for our car conversation. You inspire me so much. Thank you for allowing me into your author journey, letting me crash out on your phone at any time of day, and being someone I can count on. I am so grateful for the range of our friendship—whether we're at IKEA, celebrating "more life," or yapping when we're supposed to be writing. Plenty of years down, plenty more to go.

To my other best friends whom I met through writing, whether journalism or creative: VF, CT, RTW, KC, DJ. Thank you for growing with me in this writing game, for the endless conversations about what it means to be a writer, for being a part of my life outside of writing and sharing in all my daily ups and downs. Thank you for visiting when you can and replenishing our friendship well. It means the world.

Thank you to more best friends (yes, I have a lot of besties, I'm sorry), my support system who reminds me who I am during the writing process: KG, JO, JB. Thank you for seeing me, whether it's at brunch, during a game night, or on FaceTime as I sit at my writing desk, states away. You all ground me and continue to show me how friendship can evolve in beautiful ways. Thank you for doing life with me.

Now to the nitty-gritty. Thank you to the Sarah Lawrence MFA Writing Program and all my professors, as well as Brian Morton, Amparo Rios, and Paige Ackerson-Kiely—you all showed me what it means to carve out a writing life. And shout-out to my teachers who have honed my writing since I was a wee little thing: Mrs.

Jesse, Ms. Leyndyke, Ms. Peterson, Mrs. Barnes, and the late Mrs. Young. Thank you to the many organizations that have supported this novel: Reese's Book Club LitUp fellowship, Tin House, Kimbilio, Crosstown Arts, We Need Diverse Books, and Voyage YA.

Finally, thank you to skating rinks across the United States that allow Black people to skate and be and celebrate and love. And most of all, thank you, readers, for picking up this book. I hope it inspires you to float, glide, and soar through life with your community right by your side.